Barry picked up the ball
field. Danny had to run
the goal. He kicked it out,
flight of the ball perfectly, trapped it and brought
it down to his feet in one easy movement. He felt a
tremendous surge of excitement. It was going to be
OK. He heard the thud of feet behind him, and
something hit him hard behind the knees. He
smashed into the ground with a crunch that
knocked the breath out of him. He tried to get up
but his head was spinning and his legs were on
fire. He heard Barry say: 'You didn't have to do
that, Shane. You could have really hurt him.'

'It was a sliding tackle, that was.'

Robbie sat up. Shane was grinning all over his
stupid face. He flexed his knees carefully. They
still worked, but Shane's heavy boots had scraped
the backs of both legs raw . . .

Don't miss any of the other titles in the
top-scoring Yearling Soccer series:

BROOKSIE
by Neil Arksey

FOOTBALL MAGIC
by E. Dale

RIVERSIDE UNITED!
by Chris d'Lacey

TROUBLEMAKERS

PAUL MAY

CORGI YEARLING BOOKS

TROUBLEMAKERS
A CORGI YEARLING BOOK : 0 440 864194

First publication in Great Britain

PRINTING HISTORY
Corgi Yearling edition published 1999

Set in 13/15pt New Century Schoolbook by
Phoenix Typesetting, Ilkley, West Yorkshire

Corgi Yearling Books are published by
Transworld Publishers Ltd,
61–63 Uxbridge Road, Ealing, London W5 5SA,
in Australia by Transworld Publishers (Australia) Pty. Ltd,
20 Alfred Street, Milsons Point, NSW 2061
and in New Zealand by Transworld Publishers (NZ) Ltd,
18 Poland Road, Glenfield, Auckland.

Made and printed in Great Britain by
Cox & Wyman Ltd, Reading, Berkshire.

For Ellie, Emily and Thomas

CHAPTER 1

The crowd roared as Robbie turned and sprinted for the penalty area. He left the big defender for dead. The cross flew towards him and just when it seemed to be too late he cartwheeled backwards. His spinning right foot intersected perfectly with the flight of the ball and slammed it past the despairing fingers of the goalkeeper. There was a moment of stunned silence, then the crowd were on their feet, cheering wildly . . .

'Robbie? Come on, Robbie! I'm talking to you. Hey Robbie! Look out!' Laura grabbed Robbie's arm.

'Get off! What's the matter?'

'You were miles away. You nearly walked in front of that bus. You've been like it all day.'

They were outside the school gates. A bus full of screaming kids was pulling away. As it went, Laura saw Mr Osborne. 'Oh no,' she groaned, 'it's Ozzie.'

With his ancient tweed jacket and his corduroy trousers Mr Osborne looked like a relic from another age. But Ozzie was no joke, especially when it came to school uniform. Laura had plenty of reasons to be worried. She counted them off under her breath: knee-length red boots, black tights, red mini skirt, fluffy pink jacket . . . that meant detention at least . . . and then there was the make-up. Her heart sank. Ozzie was like a Rottweiler with a hangover after he'd done bus duty. To her amazement he ignored her completely.

'So, Robbie Devlin, eh? Not content with dreaming your way through my maths lesson you try and kill yourself by walking under the school bus. Lucky for you that your friend here had the presence of mind to stop you.'

'Yes, sir. Sorry, sir.'

'And is there some explanation for this extraordinary behaviour?'

'Not really, sir. I was just a bit tired, that's all.'

'I see. Then these, what shall we call them, illustrations? In your maths book . . .' Ozzie waved the offending document at Robbie. 'These wouldn't have anything to do with it?' Robbie felt himself reddening. Laura couldn't believe her luck. Ozzie hadn't even glanced at her clothes.

'Not exactly mathematics, is it?' Mr Osborne said. Robbie squirmed with embarrassment. His book was open in Ozzie's hand. Two pages were covered with pictures of footballers in acrobatic poses.

'I'm really sorry, Mr Osborne. I didn't realize I was doing it. I was thinking about the overhead volley, you see. The one Dino Baggio scored on Saturday. I saw it on *Match of the Day*. I watched it over and over yesterday, but I can't work out how he did it. So I was thinking . . .'

His voice tailed off. Why was he saying this? To Ozzie of all people. He stared at the ground. Laura was watching Mr Osborne closely, looking for a chance to slip away. She was astonished to see the ghost of a smile hover on his lips.

'Hmmm. Well! Perhaps in future you'll pay more attention. And don't walk under any buses on the way home.' He turned away. Laura could have sworn he was humming under his breath.

'Pinch me, will you? Tell me I'm not dreaming. Does this look like school uniform? Maybe his eyesight's going.'

'I can't believe I did that,' said Robbie. 'Going on about Dino Baggio like that. I must be crazy.'

'You said it, not me,' said Laura. 'Obsessed, that's the word I'd use. You never think about anything else. Are you coming round mine before the class?'

'I can't. Gran's taking me to see United again.'

Laura put her bag down on the pavement and stood in front of Robbie, blocking his way.

'You're giving up dancing, aren't you? Why don't you just say so?'

'I'm not . . . I mean I don't want to, it's just . . . there's no time any more.'

'Mum's really fed up, you know. She says you could be really good. And she doesn't get many boys. I wish your gran had never taken you to that match.'

'Well she did. Honest, Laura, if you could have seen it. It was just so brilliant . . .'

'Robbie! I've heard all this, remember? About a hundred times.'

Laura wasn't exaggerating. Robbie had been her best mate since the day, years before, when he had turned up at Laura's mum's dance class. He was five years old at the time, and he'd been driving his mum crazy after seeing a ballet on the TV at Christmas. All these years he'd kept going to classes, long after all the other boys had dropped out, in spite of all the stupid jokes he had to put up with at school. But then, last August, Robbie's gran had taken him to a football match, and it was as if he was five years old again. He'd turned up at Laura's the next day, his eyes shining with his new discovery.

'You should have seen it,' Robbie had said.

'I have,' said Laura. 'On TV. It's boring.'

'But it's not!' said Robbie, 'It's not like it is on TV. You can't imagine . . . there are thousands and thousands of people . . . The noise is unbelievable . . .'

It had been Chester Smith who had tipped Robbie over the edge. The game Gran had dragged Robbie along to see had been

Smith's first game for United. He was their most expensive ever signing, bought for their first season in the Premiership. In that first game he'd played like a genius, elegant and graceful as he stroked the ball around the pitch, dazzlingly fast as he sprinted from midfield to score the winning goal. In the way he moved, Robbie had seen everything he loved about dancing, and something more, something he wanted for himself . . .

Laura still stood there, angrily blocking the path.

'You're just wasting your time,' she said. 'If Mr Pitt ever puts you in the school team it'll be a miracle.'

'What do you know about it? I'm getting better all the time. You're supposed to be my friend. You should be on my side. I haven't got time for this.'

Robbie ran off down Meadow Road. He tried to push Laura's words out of his mind. He did feel bad about missing so many dance classes. It wasn't that he'd gone off dancing, only he had a lot of catching up to do.

At school he'd played football of course, in PE lessons, but he'd always played with the no-hopers. In fact, he'd always been useless on purpose, so he didn't get injured and mess up his dancing. Now that he actually wanted to play, no-one would take him seriously. He always ended up staggering around in the Bog with the useless kids. The Bog was a muddy swamp of a football pitch. It was a long way from the bright floodlights of United's North Park ground. Mr Pitt, the PE teacher, wasn't interested in the no-hopers in the Bog. He concentrated on training his 'lads'. Robbie was desperate for a chance to show Mr Pitt what he could do, but he hadn't yet managed to gather the courage to ask him.

He was nearly home. If I bounce the ball off the back wall of the house, he thought, then I can fall back on the grass and volley it into the bushes.

He'd been banned from using the garden after a number of accidental breakages. But the alley was no good for what he had in mind. It was January, and the days were short, but if he got home quickly there would still be half an hour of daylight before Mum got in from work.

By the time Mum came in Robbie was bruised and disappointed. It had looked easy on the TV. The trouble was, the ball came back so fast off the wall of the house that by the time he had begun to fall over backwards, the ball had gone.

'What are you doing, Robbie?' said Mum. 'You know you shouldn't be playing with that ball in the garden. Your dad'll murder you if he catches you. And look at that tracksuit! It had better go straight in the wash or there'll be mud everywhere.'

'It's the overhead volley, Mum. I saw it on TV. Only I can't do it without someone to help me. I need someone to throw the ball for me.'

'Why don't you play up the rec, like the other boys? Barry's up there all the time, as far as I can see.'

'Exactly,' said Robbie. 'It's more like a bloodbath up there than a game of football. Why don't you throw it, Mum? Go on, just once. Please?'

'Oh, all right, love, but you're to go straight in after, and get in the bath. How d'you want me to throw it then?' Mum put her bag down and picked up the football as if it was an unexploded bomb.

'About level with my shoulders. I face this way and you throw it across behind my back, see?'

'Like this?'

Mum threw. It was perfect. Robbie watched the ball all the way as he fell backwards. He felt as though it was happening in slow motion. He had all the time in the world. His foot met the ball with a satisfying thud. This was followed almost immediately by the crash and tinkle of exploding glass.

'I did it! I did it!' yelled Robbie, jumping up and down with excitement.

'You certainly did!' Mum exclaimed. 'That's your dad's shed window. There's glass everywhere.'

'That's the problem with overhead volleys. They said after the match. You can't always control where they end up.'

'Well you can tell that to your dad then. Maybe he'll understand what you're talking about. It won't mend that window though. Or clear up the glass.'

'Right!' said Dad, when he saw the state of his shed. 'Where's that blasted football? That's six windows now. You still haven't finished paying for the last one. You can have this back when I see the money. I told you, didn't I? No football in the garden.'

'It was only once, Dad, honest! It was really important. I was trying to do an overhead volley, and I did it, didn't I, Mum?'

'Leave me out of this, love. I don't want to know.'

'Well anyway,' Robbie continued, 'Mum threw the ball. So I thought it was all right.'

Dad looked at Mum. 'You're too soft,' he said. 'The last thing he needs is people encouraging him.'

'Oh come on, Bob. At least he cleared the glass up. And you know he hands over most of his pocket money as it is.'

'Well, you're not having it back now,' said Dad. 'This time tomorrow night, OK?'

'You can't, Dad. I've got to practise.'

'That's all you ever do,' Barry butted in. Barry was Robbie's big brother, a year older. 'You're mad, you are. Football's not just bouncing a ball up and down on your foot, you know.'

'You go from one extreme to the other,' said Dad. 'For God knows how many years it's been dancing, dancing, dancing, till we've had it coming out of our ears. Then your gran takes you to half a dozen matches and dancing's out the window. And speaking of windows, you can get that banner or whatever it is down. I mean, I support United. I always have. But I draw the line at banners hanging out of the window. It makes the place look like a tip.'

'You're not a real supporter.' Robbie felt his face getting hot. It was always like this with Dad. 'You never go to a match. You don't know anything about football!'

'Robbie!' Mum snapped. 'Don't speak to your father like that.'

'I know this much,' said Dad. 'It doesn't matter how much you practise your over-head volleys. It doesn't matter how much you practise your fancy skills. You have to be tough to play football. You have to be able to take a few knocks. You'll never get anywhere juggling a ball in the back alley. I'll believe you're serious when I see you in the school team. Maybe.'

'Bob!' said Mum, as Robbie stormed out of the room. 'You go too far sometimes, you really do!'

Robbie grabbed a tennis ball and went out into the alley. 'I hate him!' he thought. 'I wish he was dead!'

He began to kick the ball against the fence, savagely at first, left foot, right foot, left foot. Gradually he grew calmer. The alley was wide. It ran between the back gardens of the council houses. There was a street-light at each end and his breath smoked orange in the frosty air. He flicked the ball up easily. It was harder with a tennis ball. That was good. It was the same routine every night. Keep the ball off the ground all the time, ten with the right foot, ten with the left, then onto his knees, then his head. He did it loads of different ways. Keep it up. Nothing else mattered. Nothing.

Robbie didn't stop until Mum came out into the alley to fetch him in.

'You'll have to stop now, love. You're going to the match, remember. Gran'll be here in ten minutes and you haven't had your tea yet.'

'Where's Dad?'

'He's gone down the allotment. He doesn't mean half what he says, you know.'

'Then he shouldn't say it, should he?'

'He was fed up, that's all. About the window. About *all* the windows. You must admit, it was a bit daft, playing in the garden after he told you not to.'

'You'd think he'd be pleased I want to play football. He hated me dancing. He won't even give me a chance.'

'Well, you'll just have to show him, love. Get yourself in that team, then he'll sit up and take notice. Now come and get your tea.'

CHAPTER 2

'Get a move on!' said Gran. 'They won't delay the kick-off for us, you know.' Robbie's gran was small and round. Her glasses had steamed up, and she was polishing them on the end of the green-and-white scarf that was knotted around her wrist. Robbie pulled on the green-and-white hat Gran had knitted him as he swallowed a last mouthful of tea.

'Where's the banner gone, love? I was looking forward to seeing that.'

'Dad made me take it down,' said Robbie. 'He said it made the house look untidy.'

Gran snorted. 'He's his father's son, right enough. I'll have a word with him later. Are you ready?'

*　　*　　*

It was ten miles to the city from the small country town where they lived. Gran parked her battered blue Mini in a side street and they joined the steady stream of supporters making their way towards North Park. Familiar smells of hot dogs and frying onions wafted from the stalls on the street corners.

Gran had been a season-ticket holder at North Park for nearly thirty years. She'd offered to take Barry several times, but Barry was an Arsenal fan, like his friend Shane. Robbie had always been so wrapped up in his dancing that Gran had never thought of taking him. Then on a summer Saturday at the start of the season, she'd come round for lunch and found Robbie sitting around looking bored.

'Why don't you come to the match?' she'd said. 'Go on, Robbie. It can't be worse than sitting around here with nothing to do.'

'Don't make me laugh,' said Dad. 'Our Robbie at a football match! Come off it, Mum.'

That was enough for Robbie. 'OK, Gran,' he'd said, looking at Dad, 'why not?'

Everyone in Row L of the South Stand knew Gran. Everyone had a friendly word to say as they stood up to let Robbie and Gran into their seats. Below them on the pitch the teams were warming up, and Robbie watched with a mixture of excitement and dread. He couldn't understand how the players who'd been so fantastic in that first game, back at the start of the season, could be playing so badly now. They'd played well in patches, but as soon as one of them made a mistake, nervousness spread through the team like a creeping disease. It had even affected Chester Smith. He'd been outstanding in his first two games.

'You mark my words,' Gran had said, to anyone who'd listen, 'that lad'll play for England one day.'

Then, as the weeks went by, even Chester Smith had begun to make mistakes. Recently fans had begun to mutter about the money he'd cost. Robbie had defended him hotly, but now he felt as nervous before each game as if he was going to play himself.

United kicked off. Before many minutes had passed even Robbie could see that Chester Smith just didn't want the ball.

'Why's he playing on the wing, Gran?' said Robbie, pointing to Smith, close to the touchline below them. 'He's not even calling for it.'

'He doesn't want it, love. His confidence has gone.'

'But why? He's better than any of them.'

'If I knew that, love, I'd probably be managing a football team myself. Let's just pray he gets over it soon.'

The United fans were silenced by a dismal performance, and the gloom deepened when a mistake by a United defender led to Albion scoring the softest of goals.

Straight from the kick-off Albion attacked again. Their full-back brought the ball forward and ran at Chester Smith. Robbie was on his feet yelling. 'Get into him, Chester! It's yours!' Smith hesitated, then stuck out a foot and to everyone's surprise, won the ball. There was a ripple of applause around the ground as he brought it away and ran wide to Robbie's left.

He stopped for a second, trying to pick out one of the United forwards who were streaming towards the Albion penalty area. Something flew from the crowd and landed at Smith's feet. Then Robbie heard the chanting. It was coming from further along in the stand. The words made Robbie feel sick. They were aimed at Chester Smith, at the colour of his skin. They were aimed to hurt.

Robbie could almost feel Smith fighting for concentration, looking away from the crowd, lifting his boot to hit the pass; but it was too late. That brief pause and the glance into the crowd had been enough. A defender thudded into Smith and the ball cannoned into touch.

Smith got to his feet and walked towards the crowd. He seemed to be shouting something. Two policemen stepped forward and one of them grabbed Smith's arm. He shook the policeman off angrily and pointed into the crowd. The policemen went to grab him again, and Smith lashed out at the restraining arm. The referee was there, and other United players were running up now, trying to separate Smith from the police. They released him and stepped back off the pitch as the referee took his notebook out of his pocket and showed Smith a yellow card.

'But it wasn't his fault!' said Robbie indignantly. 'The police should have been telling those people to shut up, not Chester.'

'They're a disgrace, those louts,' said Gran. 'No-one should have to put up with that. If only he hadn't lost his temper; he never has before – and that won't be the worst he's had to put up with, not by a long way. Look over there. Glover's taking him off.'

Ron Glover, the United manager, was on his feet. Matt Barnson was out of the dugout, doing his sprints along the side of the pitch. As Barnson stripped off his tracksuit, Robbie saw the assistant coach holding up the number ten sign, and Chester Smith walked very slowly over the touchline and straight down the tunnel.

'Not him!' said Gran, as Barnson ran on to the field. 'That's all we need!'

The rest of the game was a disaster for United. If it hadn't been for Alex Evans in goal it would have been even worse, but as it was they lost 3−0. Thousands of fans began making their way out of the ground long before the final whistle. Gran and Robbie stayed right to the end. 'I've never left a game early, and I'm not about to start now,' said Gran.

When they walked into the front room at 15 Woodpecker Drive after a miserable journey home, *Sportsview* had already begun. 'Don't tell me the score,' said Dad, without taking his eyes off the telly. 'I see your three-million-pound man's got another chance, Robbie. Looks like he's out on the wing this time. He'll make a pig's breakfast of it, I dare say.'

'What a load of rubbish!' he said, ten minutes later. 'He's only had one kick. I thought these black players were meant to be fast.'

'He didn't get a kick because no-one passed to him,' said Robbie. 'If you ever bothered to go you'd see for yourself. You can't tell from the TV.'

'Look at that!' yelled Dad. 'He tried to attack a spectator! The police are dragging him off. Didn't I say they should never have bought him? Unbelievable!'

'Dad!' Robbie couldn't stop himself, though Gran laid a hand on his arm. 'How can you say that? And you didn't even see what happened!'

'I saw what I saw, Robbie. Good job Glover took him off before he went berserk.'

Robbie struggled to find something to say. He had the feeling he always had; nothing he said to Dad would make any difference. The door rattled the ornaments on the mantelpiece as it slammed shut behind him.

CHAPTER 3

'Right!' shouted Mr Pitt. 'All boys out on the field. My lads on this pitch here, the rest of you down the far end. You know what to do. Girls, Miss Jones is away so three times round the field, then you can practise throwing and catching on the playground. What's the matter with you lot?'

Five girls and a small boy with glasses stood in a little group clutching scraps of paper. The rest of them were shivering in their PE kit on the edge of the field. Along the fence a row of poplars bent nearly double in the biting wind. Mr Pitt didn't allow tracksuits.

'We've got notes, sir.' Laura waved her note towards him. She was wearing uniform today. No sense in pushing her luck.

'Fine,' said Mr Pitt. 'In my room then.' He ignored the note. Like the other girls, Laura had scribbled hers five minutes before. Mr Pitt never looked at them. He stood on the balls of his feet, bouncing gently, trying to look tall and failing. 'Off you go then,' he said. 'No, not you, Simpson. Come here. Let's see your note.' The small boy in glasses turned back.

'It's my asthma, sir.' He held out his note, a real one, written at breakfast-time by his anxious mother.

'Rubbish!' said Mr Pitt. 'Get yourself changed. Then you can run around the field with the girls.'

There was a murmur from the other kids.

'Please, sir,' said Robbie, 'that's William. He does get asthma, really bad. Last year he had to go to hospital. He nearly died.'

Mr Pitt's face darkened. He couldn't stand being made to look stupid. On the other hand, he couldn't afford to have the little creep die on him.

'You're pathetic!' he said to William. 'If you ask me, you need more exercise, not less. Well, go on then. You'd better do what Mummy says. In my room with the others.'

27

There were sniggers from some of the boys.

'Right! Let's get started.' Mr Pitt began to walk towards the football pitch.

'Mr Pitt. Mr Pitt?' It was that boy again. Mr Pitt stopped and turned round, trying to remember the kid's name.

'What is it now?'

Robbie's heart was thumping in his chest, but he knew he had to do this some time.

'Can I have a go with your group, Mr Pitt? I've been practising.'

Mr Pitt looked him up and down. 'I've not seen you play before, have I?'

'No, sir.'

'And you reckon you can stand up to those big lads over there? You're not exactly a big lad yourself, are you?'

Most people called Robbie skinny. They failed to notice the muscles that had grown through the years of ballet classes. Mr Pitt saw a skinny kid who wouldn't last five minutes with his lads. One crunching tackle and the kid would probably never bother him again.

'Go on, then,' he said, 'I'll give you a trial.'

Robbie had never felt so alone. Mr Pitt had given him a yellow training bib and a pair of shin-pads, and told him to play on the right side of the midfield. He stood there, feeling stupid and useless, waiting for the whistle to blow for the Reds to kick off. He heard Ian Johnstone's voice: 'You won't start dancing, will you, Robbie? Don't forget you're playing football.' Some of the others laughed and shouted at him. He felt sick. Then the whistle blew.

This was nothing like the other games Robbie had played in. Down in the Bog at least he'd had plenty of chances to kick the ball. Hardly anyone else had been interested. Here, it soon became obvious that no-one had any intention of passing to him. The match flowed on around him, but he might as well have been invisible. The Red team didn't even bother to mark him. All around him players yelled at each other, calling for the ball, shouting encouragement, and he heard Mr Pitt yelling from the touchline.

'Come on, Devlin, call for the ball, get stuck in.'

Shane Peabody ran past him, Barry's mate. 'Forget it, Robbie,' he jeered. 'Get back to your ballet lessons.'

The Yellows were attacking now: Jake Potter had the ball, out on the left wing, and

Robbie moved forward towards the edge of the penalty area, hoping that maybe Jake's cross would reach him. The ball flew into the heart of the six-yard box and Max Jenkins leapt above everyone else to punch the ball clear.

Time seemed to stand still as the ball dropped at Robbie's feet. There it was, sitting there on the grass in front of him. Players on every side were shouting at him, running towards him, and his legs felt like sacks of potatoes, huge, clumsy, impossible to move. Shane whipped the ball away from him, and he heard the groans of disappointment from the other Yellow players as their promising attack turned suddenly into desperate defence.

Robbie stood miserably, rooted to the spot, as every player on the field raced away from him.

'Go on, Rob,' called Max from his goal. 'You'll be offside if you stay there.' Robbie just had time to register the sympathy in Max's voice before he heard Mr Pitt shouting.

'Devlin! Come here.'

Robbie walked over to the touchline.

'Give us that bib, lad. I've seen enough. Get back down there with the rest of them.'

'But they wouldn't give me the ball,' said Robbie, his misery turning rapidly to anger. 'I didn't have a chance.'

'Don't tell me what happened. I saw what happened. You couldn't hack it, that's all. Off you go.'

'It's not fair,' said Robbie. 'You don't care about skill, that's what it is.'

He knew he had gone too far before the words were out of his mouth.

'You what? Right, lad. Detention. My room after school. You can run round the field till the end of the lesson.'

Robbie pounded round the field, running his anger away. Mr Pitt made people run because he thought they hated it, and some of them did, but not Robbie. He could run and run; it cleared his head. He ran past the Bog. Joe Grant was trying to shoot. He took a swing at the ball and it rolled less than a metre before sticking in the thick mud. 'I'd rather be running,' Robbie thought.

As he ran he thought about the match the night before. He still couldn't believe it. It was bad enough what had happened to Chester Smith, but then all those stupid things Dad had said about him . . . and the papers this morning, the headlines.

'SMITH'S SHAME!' it said in huge letters across the back of the *Daily Comet* that Dad was reading at breakfast.

'Look at that!' he said, triumphantly. 'There's your precious Chester Smith. The sooner they get rid of him the better. Here!' Dad took the outside of the paper and passed it over the cornflakes packet. 'Read it yourself.'

Robbie looked at the paper. 'This isn't right!' he said. 'People were chanting things at him, and . . .'

'Oh, give it a rest, Robbie. Fans always take the mickey. Players have to be able to handle it. Face it, he's useless!'

'Well I bet you wouldn't like it if they called *you* that. Gran told you, didn't she?'

'I'm not one of them though, am I? And anyway, you'd have thought he'd be used to it by now. He cost us three million quid for God's sake. A little bit of banter from the fans shouldn't put him off.'

Robbie had screwed the paper into a ball and thrown it in the bin. He'd been feeling angry ever since. He was angry now with himself for blowing his chance with Mr Pitt. He re-lived it in his mind, the way it should have been . . . *The ball came flying from Max's fist and he was ready for it . . .*

eyes fixed on the ball as his foot crashed it into the net . . .

A yell brought him back to reality as he turned to run past the football pitch yet again. Mr Pitt was joining in the match. Robbie watched him shove a couple of kids aside and smash the ball at the goalkeeper. The force of the shot took the keeper by surprise and hit him full in the face. Blood spurted from his nose, and tears of pain oozed from his eyes.

'Come on!' yelled Mr Pitt. 'Get on with the game.'

Robbie ran on.

After PE, Robbie found Laura in the corridor.

'I'll meet you outside, right?' said Laura. 'I've just got to collect some stuff from the classroom. I've got something to show you. Something you'll like.'

'I can't,' said Robbie, 'I've got a detention. From Mr Pitt.'

Laura's face fell. 'But how . . . ? I mean, you stay well out of his way, normally.'

'It doesn't matter. I'll come tomorrow. I promise.'

'Aren't you going to ask me what it is?'

'What?'

'You know, what I wanted to show you.'

'Well, you're obviously bursting to tell me,' said Robbie. Laura really knew how to wind him up. There was a smug smile on her face.

'I've got a poster,' she said, 'from a magazine. From *Tracey*.'

'Oh yeah,' said Robbie, wondering how Laura could possibly think he'd be interested. 'So what's so special about this poster then?'

'It's Chester Smith!'

'Liar!'

'I knew that'd surprise you. There was an interview with him in the magazine and you could send off for this free signed poster.'

Robbie was furious. 'What do you want a poster of Chester Smith for? You don't even like football.'

'I like him, though,' said Laura. 'He's gorgeous! Look out! Here comes Mr Pitt. Enjoy your detention!'

'Right,' grunted Mr Pitt. 'In here.' He pushed open the door of his room. As he did so a voice echoed down the corridor.

'Mr Pitt! Could I have a word with you please?' Miss MacGregor, the new head-teacher was walking towards them. Her face was pale and clear-skinned beneath her short, expensively cut red hair. Her mouth was set in a firm line, and her green eyes were angry, though her voice, with its slight Scottish accent, was cool and collected. Behind her, Robbie saw the boy who had been hit in the face by the football. His hand was squashed by the gigantic fist of his mother, a great square tank of a woman dressed all in black, and with a dangerous glint in her eye.

'Just let me at him!' she spat the words like bullets. Mr Pitt seemed to shrink.

'If we could all go to my office,' said Miss MacGregor, 'I'm sure we can sort this out sensibly.'

'Huh!' snorted the big woman, but Miss MacGregor ushered her calmly back down the corridor.

Robbie was forgotten. First good thing that's happened all day, he thought. He was halfway home when he heard the shouts from the rec. He stopped. It couldn't be any worse than what had happened in PE. The only way he'd ever stop them laughing at him was by showing them he could do it.

35

CHAPTER 4

There was always a game at the rec after school. When Robbie got there they were still arguing about the sides, hugging themselves and stamping their feet to keep warm.

'Can I have a game?' asked Robbie.'

'Tell your little brother to go away, Barry,' said Shane Peabody.

'We do need one more,' said Mike.

'Well you have him on your team then,' sniffed Shane. ''Cos me and Barry don't want him, do we, Barry? He's useless.'

Shane had been Barry's best friend for as long as Robbie could remember. Shane was in Robbie's year and Barry was in the year above. Barry had looked after Shane in the playground when Shane first started Primary school, but Shane hadn't needed looking after for long. Shane had always been big for his age, and Barry had been following Shane around ever since. That's what Robbie thought anyway. He'd never liked Shane much, and he hadn't improved with age. Barry mumbled something, but Robbie was happy. He was going to get a game.

'You go in goal then,' said Mike.

'No way!'

'Do you want to play, or not?'

'Well, OK then, but I'm not staying in all the time.'

'Yeah, sure,' said Mike.

Shane's brother, Darren, had been sitting on the swings, watching.

'What you letting him play for, Shaney? Isn't he the ballet dancer? You going soft, or what?' Darren flicked the butt of his cigarette towards Robbie. It hit the ground in a shower of sparks.

'You watch, Darren,' said Shane. 'It'll be a laugh.'

'No thanks,' said Darren, 'I got better things to do. See you later.'

Robbie stood between the piled-up coats that served as goal posts, watching the game. It was a mess. None of them had any skill. They all ran around in a frantic huddle, hacking at anything in reach. The ball ran loose and Mike kicked wildly at it. It looped towards Barry in the other goal, but Barry was gazing at an aeroplane passing overhead and the ball rolled gently over the goal line. Shane had a go at Barry.

'What's going on?' Robbie asked, walking down the pitch.

'Get back in goal,' said Mike.

'Why can't someone else go in? I've had enough.'

'You're a pain,' grumbled Mike.

'I told you,' Shane said.

'Go on then, Danny, you go in,' Mike decided, picking on the smallest boy. Danny groaned. Barry picked up the ball and belted it down the field. Danny had to run to stop it bouncing into the goal. He kicked it out, and Robbie, judging the flight of the ball perfectly, trapped it and brought it down to his feet in one easy movement. He felt a tremendous surge of excitement. It was going to be OK. He heard the thud of feet behind him, and something hit him hard behind the knees. He smashed into the ground with a crunch that knocked the breath out of him. He tried to get up but his head was spinning and his legs were on fire. He heard Barry say: 'You didn't have to do that, Shane. You could have really hurt him.'

'It was a sliding tackle, that was.'

Robbie sat up. Shane was grinning all over his stupid face. He flexed his knees carefully. They still worked, but Shane's heavy boots had scraped the backs of both legs raw. He fought back tears of pain and rage. He wouldn't let them beat him. He stood up.

'It's our free kick, then,' he said. 'I'll take it.'

'That was never a foul,' said Shane. 'I told you, it was a sliding tackle.'

'Shut up, Shane,' said one of the others. 'Let him take it if he wants to.'

'That's right,' said Mike. 'Our free kick.'

'OK,' said Shane. 'We'll make a wall.' Robbie placed the ball. Shane and two of his mates stood in a line, far too close. 'Let them,' Robbie said to himself. He knew exactly what he was going to do. He'd practised free kicks endlessly in the alley. He stepped up and hit the ball with the outside of his left foot. It sizzled past Shane's nose and curved like a banana just inside the post. Shane couldn't believe his eyes.

'Over the post!' he said.

'No it wasn't,' said Barry, astonished. 'It was in! It was brilliant! Didn't you see it curve? And it went like a bullet.'

'That was just luck,' said Shane. 'Anyone could do it.'

'Go on then,' said Barry, 'you have a go.'

'I don't feel like it,' said Shane, 'and I've had enough of this game too. I'm not playing with a wimp like him. He was nearly crying. I saw him. You coming, Barry? Or are you going home with your little brother?'

'Well . . . yeah, all right. Are you OK, Robbie?'

'I'm fine,' Robbie lied, gritting his teeth. 'Leave us the ball. I want to practise.'

'You ought to go home,' said Barry. 'It's getting dark.'

'Come on, Barry. Just leave him. That's what he wants. You heard.'

For a moment, as the voices faded, Robbie regretted staying behind. The rec was kind of eerie with nobody there, and the sky fading from red to green as the sun disappeared. He wanted to take some corners; practise curling the ball into the near post, making it hang in the air just out of reach of where the keeper would be. The old white goal posts down the far end were perfect. He didn't notice the man sitting quietly on the bench behind the goal, and he hit the ball far harder than he intended. It smacked into the side of the man's head before he could move. He stood up.

'I'm really sorry.' Robbie was horrified. 'I didn't see you there. I didn't mean to . . . I mean, I was just taking a corner, but there wasn't anyone there to head it in so it sort of . . . came over here and hit you . . .' He ran out of words, finally. There was something about the man . . . He was wearing an old anorak and a moth-eaten woolly hat, but his face . . . Robbie looked again. The man's mouth was open and his eyes were wide, surprised.

'But you're Chester Smith!'

'Never mind me,' said Chester Smith. 'How on earth did you do that?'

CHAPTER 5

'It is you, isn't it?' said Robbie.

'Yeah, worse luck,' said Chester. 'I just wanted some space; time to think; but you've wrecked that, haven't you? You're not supposed to recognize me in this gear either.'

'It was an accident, honest,' said Robbie. 'I couldn't help it. I only . . .'

'OK, OK,' said Chester. 'I was joking, right? Calm down.'

'But why don't you want anyone to recognize you?'

'Are you kidding? After last night? I needed to think . . . without reporters breathing down my neck. I just wanted to get away . . .'

There was a silence. Robbie looked sideways at Chester's face. He was staring miserably at a small patch of grass by his feet.

'We were at the match last night,' said Robbie. 'Me and my gran. We saw what happened.'

'Oh yeah? "SMITH'S SHAME". That what you saw?'

'No!'

'Seems to be what everyone else saw.'

'I heard what they were shouting. And anyway, you never got anywhere near them.'

'Well, thanks,' said Chester. 'Look, it's been going round and round in my head all day. I've had enough of thinking. Why don't you take some more corners, only this time I'll be ready.' He rubbed the side of his face where the ball had hit him. 'If you can hit a few more like that I'll be seriously impressed. I might even be able to forget that I've wrecked my career, just for a few minutes.'

'But you haven't . . .'

'I told you, I don't want to talk about it. You want to play or not?'

'You mean it?' said Robbie. 'Really?'

'Sure,' said Chester. 'The one that hit me

43

was just begging to be headed into the net. I told you, I want to see if you can do it again. But you haven't told me your name.'

'It's Robbie. Robbie Devlin.'

'Chester Smith, at your service.' Chester stood up and held out his hand. Robbie shook it. *This can't be happening*, he told himself.

'OK,' said Chester, 'let's get on with it.'

Twenty minutes later Barry walked past the rec on his way home. He noticed the odd-looking couple kicking a ball around by the old goal posts, but then he saw the plane, high overhead, glinting silver in the sunset. By the time he had watched it shrink to a tiny black dot, Barry was nearly home. Then he remembered the man and the kid at the rec. There was something odd about them. That kid could have been Robbie. What was he doing playing around with a stranger in the rec? It was almost dark. Dad would know what to do. Barry began to run.

Chester and Robbie were having a good time. It was weeks since Chester had enjoyed kicking a football. He'd forgotten how good it felt, just kicking a ball backwards and forwards in a park. And this kid was brilliant. Chester felt a shiver of excitement run through him. This must be what the scout had felt, who'd first spotted Andy Cole, or Michael Owen. *Don't be daft*, he told himself, *you're imagining it*, but as they played on he became more and more convinced. The kid had fantastic balance and terrific co-ordination, and he was strong; he could hit the ball an amazingly long way for someone who looked so skinny. There was no doubt in his mind: Robbie was the real thing – raw talent.

'Can you do overhead volleys?' said Robbie when they stopped for a moment.

'What do you mean, "Can I?" Of course I can. I'm the best.'

'Will you show me? I mean, show me how?'

'Sure. No problem. Cross the ball, about here.' Robbie hit a cross so perfect he could hardly believe his own eyes. Chester blurred into movement, and the ball rocketed into the top right-hand corner of the goal.

'I don't understand,' Robbie said. 'You can do that, so easily, but last night, you looked like you didn't even want to touch the ball.'

'I thought we weren't going to talk about it,' Chester replied, picking himself up and brushing the mud from his trousers.

'I want to know,' said Robbie. 'Those people at the match, was it them? Is that why you started making mistakes?'

'What am I supposed to say?' Chester was angry. 'All my life I've put up with that kind of rubbish. If you're black and you want to play football you ignore it – if you want to get anywhere, that is. You get it from other players; you get it from the crowd, but you can't *retaliate*. That's what they call it. When I'm playing well, it's easy. I don't even hear it. But now . . .'

'But all those goals you scored, and the way you hit that volley . . .'

'It's one thing doing it on your own, just for yourself, doing it for fun. You wait till you've got thousands of people watching you, all waiting for you to make a mistake.'

Robbie remembered what had happened to him earlier, at school. It was bad enough with just a few other kids watching.

Chester talked on. Now he'd started he didn't seem able to stop. It was as if he was talking to himself, thinking out loud.

'I miss my mates,' he was saying, 'and I miss my mum and dad. I miss living in London, going out on the town, having a good time. It's dead around here. Maybe that's what's made me lose my edge. And when things start going wrong it just gets worse. You hit one bad pass, and before you even get the ball again you're worrying you're going to mess up. I never thought it would happen to me, but it has. Maybe I should go back to London. Or I could go to Italy, or Spain. That's what I've always wanted.'

'But you can't!' said Robbie. 'We need you. We'll never stay up without you. It's not fair.'

In a few short months Robbie had become as passionate about United as his gran.

'You expect life to be fair? I don't see anyone treating you too fair. Look at your legs. That kid could have broken them. Why are you wasting your time playing with them?'

'I don't have much choice,' said Robbie bitterly. 'No-one takes me seriously.' Before he knew what he was doing he was pouring all his problems out to Chester. The dancing, the taunts at school, Laura, Barry, Shane, Mr Pitt . . . 'And then, when I did get the chance, I just froze,' he said. 'It was terrible.'

Chester started to laugh, then he saw Robbie's face and stopped. 'Ballet!' he said.

'That explains a whole lot of things. You know, loads of clubs have ballet classes for their players nowadays, especially on the continent. I've thought about it myself. I've seen those guys jump – the ballet dancers – incredible! Be dynamite in the box. But I can't believe you've only been playing a few months. You're putting me on? Why did you suddenly start?'

Robbie was embarrassed. 'Because of you,' he said. 'Your first game at United was the first one I ever went to. That goal you scored, the second one, where you beat two defenders and curled it into the top corner – it was like you danced round them . . . it was . . .' Robbie stopped, lost for words.

Chester could see in Robbie's face that he felt just the same way about football that he did. 'Sounds like this Mr Pitt of yours didn't give you much of a chance,' he said. 'Why don't you try again. The man must have eyes.'

'I don't think so,' said Robbie.

'Well, how about your mum and dad? There must . . .'

'Mum!' gasped Robbie. 'She'll kill me! Look! It's nearly dark. they'll be going crazy!'

'Don't worry. I'll take you home and

48

explain. And I promise you, if there's anything I can do to help you play football, then I'll do it. OK?'

'Thanks,' said Robbie, 'but I'm not sure that's such a good idea. Taking me home, I mean. It's Dad, you see . . .' Robbie faltered, reddening in the darkness, remembering all the things Dad had said about Chester the night before. 'The thing is, he's . . . Hey, what's happening?'

Headlights blinded them as a car swung in through the gates at the far end of the rec and drove across the field towards them.

'Quick!' said Chester. 'Get out of the way. They're probably joy-riders.'

The car stopped a few metres away from them. Dad jumped out.

'Robbie! Get in the car! You should have been home an hour ago. You must have a screw loose. What on earth's going on here?'

'I'm sorry, Dad. I just forgot the time, that's all. Anybody would've done . . .'

'Mr Devlin,' said Chester, 'it's my fault, really.'

'Who on earth are you?' Dad snapped. 'You ought to be locked up, hanging around kids' playgrounds at this time of night.'

'Dad!' said Robbie. 'He's Chester Smith. The footballer.'

'Oh yeah, and I'm Alan Shearer,' said Dad. 'Just get in the car, Robbie, and stop making things worse.'

'But he is,' Robbie insisted.

Chester held out his hand, smiling. 'It's a long story,' he said. 'This boy's going to be a great footballer.'

Dad stared at him. There was a silence. 'To tell you the truth,' he said, finally, 'I don't really care who you are. You should have had more sense. His mum's at home, worried sick. Robbie, get in the car.'

They drove off, leaving Chester standing alone in the middle of the deserted playground.

CHAPTER 6

'What's up with you then?' asked Laura the next morning. She was waiting for Robbie at the end of Woodpecker Drive. 'Detention can't have been that bad.'

'Leave me alone,' said Robbie. He hadn't slept much. He hadn't spoken a word to anyone since Dad had driven him home the night before. Not much chance of Chester helping him now, not after what Dad had said to him. It was like somebody giving you a present and then snatching it away again before you could even start to unwrap it. As they had driven away from the rec a white car had nearly collided with them. Robbie had seen two men jump out and run over to Chester. He had seen the cameras flash. So

Chester hadn't even escaped from the reporters. That was his fault too. He'd never see him again. He walked faster.

'Oh, come on, Robbie. I'm supposed to be your friend, remember. Slow down. I can't keep up with you in these.' Laura's boots were black and shiny. They had a two-inch heel and she was clattering along behind Robbie like a lame donkey.

'Yeah? Well that's your problem, isn't it?' They walked on in silence until they came to the school gates. Then Robbie said, 'Anyway, if I told you, you'd never believe me.'

'Go on, then.'

'You won't laugh?'

'I promise.'

'I met Chester Smith last night.'

'You mean you saw him, in a car or something?'

'No.' Robbie paused. 'It sounds stupid now. I knew you wouldn't believe me.'

'Well,' said Laura, 'I haven't got all day. Are you going to tell me or not?'

'It was up the rec.' The words came out in a rush. 'I played football with him.'

Laura stared at him. 'You had a detention last night. With Mr Pitt.'

'He let me off. He had to go and see Miss

MacGregor, so I didn't have to stay. I went up to the rec to play football and after the others had gone, he was there. Chester Smith.'

'Robbie! Get real. I mean, I know what you're like when you get stuck on something, but don't you think this is taking it too far? I'm not impressed.'

'You two! Stop right there.' Mr Osborne scurried across the playground. He could move surprisingly fast when he wanted to.

'You again!' he said to Laura. 'You can't come to school dressed like that!'

'This is my school uniform, sir.'

As well as the boots, Laura was wearing a very short black skirt, black tights, and a black leather jacket.

'I fail to see . . .'

'Black or brown shoes, sir. Black or navy tights or socks. Black or navy skirt or trousers. Black or navy jacket, sir. Isn't that right, sir?'

'Hmmph!' snorted Mr Osborne, 'You know as well as I do, young lady, that leather jackets are not permitted.'

'It's not leather, sir. It's plastic!'

'Leather, plastic, it's the look of the thing that matters. Don't you see, we can't have pupils from Field View School going about looking like a gang of roughnecks. And I'm sure I remember a rule about lipstick. Remove it before school commences, please. I shall see you both in maths, and there will be no lipstick in evidence. Are you all right, young man?' Robbie looked as miserable as he felt. He nodded at Mr Osborne, who was looking at him with concern. 'If you're sure,' the teacher said doubtfully. Robbie nodded again. 'Well, I hope you feel better in time for my lesson this afternoon. I've given some special thought to your particular interests.' He was gone as quickly as he had arrived.

Laura looked at Robbie's face. 'I'm sorry,' she said, 'but you were just saying it to wind me up, weren't you?'

'I said you wouldn't believe me.'

'You mean it's true? You really met him?' Robbie nodded. 'But what's wrong? I mean, you should be over the moon. I was when I saw Jarvis Cocker in the back of a car last year, and I wasn't even absolutely sure it was him.'

'It was terrible. First I hit him on the head with my ball, but that turned out all right, only it was getting dark and Barry went and got Dad, and Dad was just so stupid and . . .'

'It was a good job I *did* get Dad,' said

Barry, coming up behind them. Shane was with him. They had walked across the playground specially.

'You're off your nut, you are!' said Shane Peabody to Robbie. 'Barry told us. Kicking a ball around with some black dosser, then you tell everyone it was Chester Smith. You're cracking up.'

'It *was* him,' said Robbie. 'Tell him, Barry. You know it was. You must have heard Dad.' Barry shook his head.

'Come on, Barry,' said Shane. 'Leave them. It's not worth it.'

Laura looked after them in disgust, then she turned back to Robbie. 'I'm sorry,' she said, 'I should have known you wouldn't make up a story like that.'

'It doesn't matter,' said Robbie. 'He said he'd help me. Now there's no chance.'

By the time afternoon school began, Robbie had stopped feeling sorry for himself and had begun to be angry. Dad's voice seemed to fill his head, trying to tell him what to think, what to be, what to do: full of opinions, some of them stupid, some of them just plain wrong. Robbie had a warm memory of Dad carrying him up to bed, tucking him and reading him a story. It was as if dancing had made a wall between them. Dad had always hated it. He'd gone on and on at Mum, telling her it was stupid letting a boy go to dancing lessons, but Mum had simply carried on taking him, twice a week, year after year. Robbie felt guilty suddenly. He'd have to go to the class tonight – explain to Laura's mum. He'd been putting it off too long . . .

'Well now, Robbie Devlin! A penny for your thoughts. I hope you're not going to make a habit of daydreaming your way through my lessons. I think you might find this one worth staying awake for.'

'Sorry, Mr Osborne.' Robbie tried to look as if he knew what was going on. Shane Peabody muttered something to one of his mates and they all sniggered.

'Be quiet, over there. Perhaps you'd like to share the joke with the rest of us? No? Fine. Now, I've noticed that some of you take a certain amount of interest in football.' Someone at the back shouted 'Uni-TED', and everyone laughed. 'Well I wonder if you've considered football from a mathematical point of view?' There were loud groans. 'No, no! It's really very fascinating. I'm sure you can think of some examples.'

'You've got to be able to read the numbers on their backs, sir!' There was more laughter. 'And count the goals!'

'Well that's a start,' said Mr Osborne, 'but . . .' There was a knock on the door and a very small boy came in.

'Please, sir, Miss MacGregor says can Robbie Devlin go to her office please?'

'Ah! So you're the mysterious Robbie Devlin!' Miss MacGregor had only arrived at Christmas, and she had not met Robbie before. Robbie was trying desperately to work out what he'd done wrong. Miss MacGregor smiled at him. 'Sit down,' she continued. 'I've just had a rather extra-ordinary telephone conversation, and your name was mentioned.'

'My name? But why? I haven't . . .'

'The person who phoned told me he was Chester Smith – a footballer, apparently. I must say, I found this very hard to believe, but he told me a remarkable story about a young boy with a lot of talent. He tells me he's phoned every school in Rexford.'

'But what did he want?' said Robbie.

'He wanted to offer us some free coaching. In his spare time, he said.'

'But what did you say? Did you say yes?'

In his excitement and relief, Robbie forgot he was talking to his headteacher.

'Do you think I should?'

'Oh, yes! He's great. It'll be brilliant.'

'So it's true then, this amazing story that he told me, about meeting you on a children's playground?'

'Did he say anything else?' Robbie asked. 'Apart from about meeting me?' The image of Dad shouting at Chester flashed across Robbie's mind.

'Only that you had to leave in a hurry and he never found out where you went to school. But you clearly made an impression; and I must say, he sounded a very nice young man, but it seems he's been in some kind of trouble.'

'It wasn't his fault! He didn't do anything wrong. I was there at the match. I saw.'

'Don't worry,' Miss MacGregor continued. 'I made some enquiries, naturally. You'll be pleased to know that the Football Association is not taking the stories in the newspapers very seriously.'

'You mean you rang them?' Robbie was astonished.

'Why not? Go right to the top, that's my motto. And I spoke to a quite extraordinary man at the football club by the name of Ron

Glover. I had a certain amount of difficulty understanding him, but anyway, he seems to feel that coaching youngsters might do Mr Smith some good. So I shall ring Mr Smith at once. Would you like to wait while I do so?'

Robbie's head was spinning. He listened in a daze as Miss MacGregor spoke to Chester and arranged a whole series of coaching sessions.

'There we are,' she said. 'What a marvellous opportunity! Mr Pitt will be delighted, I'm sure. I'll ask him to put up a notice after school.'

'Mr Pitt!?'

'Why, yes. He's in charge of PE after all. We must do things properly.'

'But he won't . . . I mean, will *anyone* be able to come?'

'But of course! Mr Smith even suggested that I see if I can find some girls who are interested. I propose to take charge of that side of things myself, as Miss Jones is ill. I can't tell you how I'm looking forward to it. And your Mr Smith will be bringing the Press too. It's really very good of him. I foresee some excellent publicity for the school.'

*   *   *

When Mr Pitt saw the crowd waiting to sign up for Chester's coaching sessions, he was baffled. Miss MacGregor had told him about Chester's offer but he had assumed that Chester would be working with his lads, and he hadn't bothered to listen to everything she said to him.

'Just hold on a minute. I can see you're all excited, but there's no way me and Chester Smith can deal with this number of people on our own. I'm sorry, but I shall have to restrict participation to those already training in my team squads.'

There were groans from the crowd. Robbie spoke up.

'Sir, Miss MacGregor said anyone could play.'

'You must have misheard.'

'Not at all, Mr Pitt,' said Miss MacGregor as she entered the room. 'Everything is in hand. Several members of staff are going to help. I did explain to you earlier, you know. Now then, I think you should be the first to sign up, Robbie. Come along.'

Mr Pitt shook his head in disbelief as Robbie stepped forward. His eyes nearly popped out when he saw Laura signing up for Miss MacGregor's group.

'You'd better make sure all these children are correctly equipped, Miss MacGregor. I'm telling you, if anything goes wrong, I certainly won't be held responsible.'

CHAPTER 7

When school was over an excited crowd gathered around Robbie, asking questions about Chester Smith. Everyone ignored Shane and Barry and their mates, but as the crowd broke up, Shane couldn't resist one last dig.

'It won't do you any good,' he sneered at Robbie. 'You're a rubbish footballer. Coaching won't change that. Doesn't matter who does it. You want to stick to ballet.' Shane did a little twirl. It usually got a laugh, but not today.

'There's nothing wrong with dancing,' said Robbie. 'That's where I'm going now. You ought to try it.' That did raise a laugh, and Shane's face darkened. He stumped off angrily across the playground.

Robbie walked along Blackbird Way with a small bunch of girls.

'What are you doing signing up for football coaching?' said Robbie to Laura. 'You don't like football.'

'I like him though, don't I?' said Laura. 'I'm not going to miss a chance like this.'

'We'll see him in the flesh,' added Laura's friend Emma. 'Do you think he'll be wearing shorts?'

'Oh, come on,' said Robbie. 'Who cares what he's wearing?'

'What are *we* going to wear?' asked Stacey. 'That's the thing. I think I'll wear my new Reeboks and my Adidas trousers.'

'But it'll be muddy,' said Laura. 'I don't want to get good stuff all dirty.'

Robbie laughed. 'I think we've got some old football boots at home,' he said. 'I'll have a look if you like.'

Robbie hadn't been to a dance class for weeks. Laura's mum used an old church hall for the classes, and when Robbie walked in she was so pleased to see him that he felt ashamed.

Laura's mum was a more extreme version of Laura with wild red hair and a bizarre assortment of leotards, cardigans, leggings and socks that she seemed to throw on at random. She'd been a professional dancer, forced by injury to give up. She was a terrific teacher.

'Well,' she said, 'the stranger returns.'

'I've been meaning to come,' said Robbie, 'only . . .'

'You don't have to say anything, Rob. The moment I saw your face after you'd been to that match, I knew I'd lost you. If you want to be a footballer, you go for it. Don't tear yourself apart trying to do two things badly.'

'But I still want to come to classes,' said Robbie. 'That is OK, isn't it? Some football clubs have ballet coaches. Did you know?'

'Sure,' said Laura's mum. 'Only, no-one's asked me yet. We'd better get started. Come on.'

After weeks without dancing, Robbie found the class hard work, and he could already feel his muscles stiffening as he ran home. When he got in he remembered his promise to Laura.

'Have you seen Barry's old football boots, Mum?'

The kitchen table was covered with books and pieces of paper. Mum was studying for an English 'A' level and she had an essay to finish. She did more homework than Robbie and Barry put together.

'What do you want football boots for?' she asked. 'You've got some, haven't you?'

'They're for Laura. She wants to learn to play. I said I'd look.'

'Laura!' Mum looked baffled. 'Oh well, I suppose you know what you're talking about. I think they're in the cupboard under the stairs.'

Robbie found the boots at last, buried under a pile of old magazines. He'd just started cleaning the mud off them when Barry came in.

'Hey! What are you doing with them?'

'I thought I could lend them to someone.'

'They're mine!'

'Yeah, but you don't wear them any more, do you? They're too small.'

'That doesn't mean I don't want them. It doesn't mean you can just take my things without asking. You've caused enough trouble already.'

'Me!' Robbie was amazed. 'What trouble

have I caused? You're the one who tried to pretend I was making it all up about Chester Smith. Shane didn't like it when he found out, did he? It serves you right! You should've been on my side when they were laughing at me.'

'Well, you needn't think it's going to make any difference to you, him doing coaching. Shane told me what happened when Mr Pitt gave you a game. You were useless.'

'That's not fair! He never gave me a proper chance. You saw that free kick I took, up at the rec.'

'That was a fluke. But it doesn't matter anyway. Shane says it's only the people in Mr Pitt's squad who'll get in the team. And Chester Smith's no good anyway.'

'Oh yeah? I suppose that's what Shane says too? What's Chester Smith ever done to him to make him talk like that? I can't believe you listen to that rubbish.'

'It's not rubbish,' Barry shouted. 'It's true! Shane says if we let blacks play there won't be any room for English people. He knows. His dad couldn't get a job where they lived before because of all the blacks. They ended up being the only white people in their street. That's why they moved here.' Barry was very red in the face.

'So now you hate black people too? You seriously believe what Shane tells you? Shane's dad couldn't get a job anywhere! What's the difference between you and someone with a black skin? There isn't any. You know where Chester was born? London, that's where. He's as English as Shane is. And anyway,' Robbie finished, 'you don't even want to be a footballer.'

'No, but Shane does. And he says there're so many black players in the top clubs that they're not even interested in looking at kids like us.'

'No-one would look at Shane because he's no good,' said Robbie.

'That's not what Mr Pitt says. Mr Pitt's a scout for United.'

'Oh yeah?'

'He thinks Shane's really good. He told him so.'

'I don't believe this!' said Robbie. 'I never thought you could be so stupid.'

'Stupid yourself!' shouted Barry, trying to snatch a boot out of Robbie's hand. 'Give me that!'

'What's going on?' called Mum. 'I can't hear myself think.'

'He's trying to nick my old football boots,' said Barry.

'Well you don't really need them any more, do you, love? It can't do any harm for one of his friends to use them.'

'One of his friends! Just because Chester Smith's coming, suddenly everyone wants to play football.'

'What are you talking about?' said Mum. 'Isn't he the one who . . . ? What's going on, Robbie?'

'He's going to come and do coaching at the school. Miss MacGregor had me in her office and told me specially, so it must be all right. I will be able to go, won't I, Mum. I don't care what Dad thinks of Chester.'

'Oh, really?' said Dad. 'What is all this? I've had it up to here with all this arguing. It's football again, isn't it?'

He had come in, unnoticed, while Robbie was talking. Gran had arrived at the same time, flushed and excited.

'Funny you should mention football,' said Gran. 'Look what just arrived! Two tickets for the Cup match at Wanderers! I thought they weren't going to arrive in time. Robbie can come with me. It'll be his first away match!'

'Over my dead body!' said Dad. 'The last thing he needs is you encouraging him, Mum. You know what happened last night.

He needs to learn his lesson. You heard him just now. He pays no attention to me. None!'

'Maybe he'd pay more attention if you made sense sometimes,' snapped Gran. 'From what you've told me you were unforgivably rude to that young man.'

'I did what any father would have done. Anything might have happened.'

'You didn't even listen to what your own son was saying. Don't you think he'd have told you if there'd been anything wrong? You haven't got the brains you were born with.'

'Chester was trying to explain, but Dad wouldn't listen,' said Robbie.

'That's my boy,' said Gran. 'Talks first, thinks afterwards, if he thinks at all.'

'I don't have to listen to this,' Dad muttered.

'Oh, yes you do!' said Gran, 'You've got a lovely family and you try to push them around like you're Adolf flamin' Hitler. You grumble about Liz doing her 'A' levels, and you moan about Barry spending all his time on his computer. So what if Robbie *has* broken a few windows? He's paying for them, isn't he? I suppose you never broke a window in your life? And then this nonsense about Chester Smith. If it had been Michael

Owen in the rec it would have been a different story, wouldn't it? And another thing . . .'

'Right!' said Dad. 'I don't suppose there's any tea. No? Well I'm going down the pub. You go to your precious football match if you like, Robbie. Obviously no-one around here gives a hoot about what I think.'

CHAPTER 8

Chester Smith walked into Field View Middle School and his heart sank. Standing in the silent corridor outside the head-teacher's office brought back bad memories. He had spent too much time waiting in corridors like this, listening to the distant classroom noises, wondering what would happen next, expecting the worst.

Chester knocked, and the door opened. He found his hand grasped in a firm, dry handshake.

'Well now, Mr Smith, this is tremendously kind of you.'

Chester realized he was staring. Miss MacGregor was young, and very good-looking. 'No, really,' he murmured. 'Like I said on the phone, I'd like to help.'

'Well, we're very grateful. We've had the most tremendous response from the children. You do seem to be very popular, and a surprising number of members of staff have volunteered to help. Even Miss Jones has struggled in from her sick bed, so there'll be two of us to work with the girls. I've arranged for all our helpers to meet here immediately after school.'

'You, er, looked at the stuff I sent you?' said Chester. 'The plans. Were they . . . OK?'

'I was impressed,' replied Miss Mac-Gregor. 'You seem tremendously well organized.'

'To tell you the truth,' said Chester, 'I got our coach to tell me what to do. I've never done anything like this before. I couldn't believe it when you told me how many kids were coming.'

Miss MacGregor looked at him, and saw that beneath the smiling exterior he was actually terrified.

'Don't worry,' she said briskly. 'I shall organize the children – and we have these excellent plans. It will all go like clockwork, you'll see.' There was a knock on the door. 'Good. Here are our assistants now, if I'm not mistaken.'

The door opened and Miss Jones limped in, assisted by Mr Osborne. They were followed by several other teachers, all of whom shook hands enthusiastically with Chester.

After the meeting, Miss MacGregor escorted Chester to the gym. Mr Pitt had not appeared yet.

'I expect he is sorting out the equipment,' explained the headteacher. 'No doubt as a qualified coach he felt he didn't need to be present.'

Something in the way Miss MacGregor said this made Chester look closely at her, but she changed the subject.

'By the way,' she continued, 'you did mention the press. Did you bring them with you?'

'They said they'd be here, but you never can tell. It's the national press, though: the *Daily Comet*.'

In the gym, Mr Pitt was waiting. He had half a dozen boys with him.

'Mr Pitt, this is Chester Smith, but then I don't suppose you need me to tell you that.'

'Pleased to meet you, lad,' said Mr Pitt, shaking Chester's hand. 'I've got some big, strong boys here, and with your help we should be able to put the finishing touches to them. I . . . er . . . have been able to recommend one or two lads to top-class clubs in the past, you know.'

'Right,' said Chester. 'Great. These are some of your lads, then?' Barry was there, and Shane. They shuffled uneasily and looked at the floor. A couple of them looked familiar to Chester: the tall blond-headed lad with the sullen face, he was the one who'd been playing in the park with Robbie that night – the chopper.

'You'd better hurry up and get changed, boys,' said Miss MacGregor. 'Mustn't waste time.' Shane turned away without speaking. The others followed him out of the gym.

Somewhere else, thought Chester. I've seen him somewhere else as well. But Miss MacGregor was talking now, very businesslike.

'Take Mr Smith over, please, Mr Pitt. Show him the equipment and make sure he has everything he needs.'

'Over here.' Mr Pitt opened the door to the PE store. 'I've sorted out the balls for us to use with the lads. They're over there: balls, set of training bibs, cones. As for the rest of them, they'll just have to make do with these. To tell you the truth, I don't know what she was thinking about just throwing it open to anyone like that. Waste of your talents if you ask me.'

Chester looked in dismay at the baskets of balls. He could see at a glance that half of them were worn out.

'They can't use these!' he said. 'Miss MacGregor said you had enough for everyone.'

He caught sight of a glint of white behind a stack of athletics equipment. He shoved some hurdles out of the way.

'What are you doing?'

Chester lifted a pile of rugby shirts. Underneath were several boxes of brand new footballs. 'What's wrong with these?' asked Chester.

'You can't use them. They're . . . they're match balls . . . they're not for practice.'

'Why don't we check with Miss MacGregor?'

'It's nothing to do with her, that's why.'

Miss MacGregor appeared in the doorway. 'Nothing to do with who, Mr Pitt? I'm pleased to see you've fetched the new balls out for us. Will you take them outside for Mr Smith, please. Oh, and I think we'll need that box of shin-pads; it's over there under that pile of cricket bats.'

Mr Pitt stared at Miss MacGregor as Chester placed a box of balls in his hands. Chester smiled.

'Thanks for your help, Mr Pitt,' he said.

Mr Pitt struggled outside with the last of the balls. He was red in the face and puffing like a steam engine.

'What's going on? There are cones everywhere. They're all over my pitch.'

'If you had bothered to come to the meeting, Mr Pitt, you would have heard me explain everything. However, as you are an expert, I'm sure this will be all you'll need,' Miss MacGregor said, handing Mr Pitt a clipboard with a couple of sheets of paper on it.

He looked at it for a few moments, then snorted. 'Kids' stuff. My lads don't need to bother with this nonsense. They need to get stuck into a decent game.'

'Mr Pitt, a top professional footballer has offered us his help with coaching our children. He is in charge. If you don't feel able to assist then I'm sure you have lessons to plan for tomorrow.'

'You . . . I . . . He . . .'

'It's up to you, Mr Pitt, go or stay, but we

really must be getting on. We don't want to disappoint the children, do we? If you look at your schedule you'll see we have five minutes' jogging first. Come along, if you're coming.'

Miss MacGregor set off, with Mr Pitt following reluctantly in her wake.

The jogging and the warm-ups settled Robbie's nerves. He'd been dreading the embarrassment of Chester singling him out, but Chester seemed to have other things on his mind. When they'd finished warming up, Miss MacGregor called them all together.

'I know you're all very grateful to Mr Smith for helping us out like this.' Chester shuffled uneasily from one foot to the other. 'Would you like to say a few words before we begin, Mr Smith?'

'Oh,' Chester mumbled. 'Right . . . I . . . Well, you know . . . Thanks.' Chester was finding forty kids just as frightening as a crowd of forty thousand. 'I, er . . .'

Miss MacGregor rescued him. 'Now then, everyone. This is a training session. Nice simple exercises designed to improve your skills.'

'Aren't we having a game then, miss?' called a voice from the back.

'Not today,' said Miss MacGregor. 'That's right, isn't it, Mr Smith?'

Chester nodded. Robbie heard the beginnings of muttering from some of the kids nearby. Mr Pitt looked as if he was about to speak, but he didn't.

'Very well,' continued Miss MacGregor. 'Let's get started.'

Robbie heard Mr Osborne call his name. His heart sank when he heard him call Shane's name too, but before he had time to worry, Mr Osborne was organizing them around the edge of a square to play piggy-in-the-middle.

'This is a kids' game,' said Shane. 'It's pointless.'

'Let's just see how well you get on, shall we?' said Mr Osborne. 'Mr Smith tells me they even do this on the United training ground sometimes.'

Max was in the middle first, racing backwards and forwards, trying to intercept the ball as the players around the edge attempted to control it quickly and pass it before he could reach them. Max was quick. Trevor passed to Shane, and Shane's control was sloppy. The ball hit his foot and bounced back. Max was on it in a flash.

'In the middle, Shane,' said Mr Osborne.

'He hit it too hard,' Shane grumbled. 'Trevor ought to go in.'

'Don't argue, Shane. Just get on with it.'

Shane stumped into the middle and the passing began again, faster now, as they tried to think and move more quickly. Very soon, Robbie realized he was getting better. In fact, they were all improving, and Shane was red in the face and out of breath. He stopped, hands on hips. 'I'm sick of this,' he complained. 'It must be someone else's turn.'

'One final effort,' said Mr Osborne. 'Come along now.'

The ball was at Trevor's feet. Shane hurled himself across the square and slid in towards Trevor, feet first. Trevor saw him coming, flicked the ball to Max, and jumped neatly over Shane's legs. Shane found himself looking up into Chester's face.

'See?' said Chester to the group. 'The great thing about being able to control and pass the ball quickly is it helps you to keep out of trouble. That was dangerous,' he said to Shane. 'Don't do it again.'

'You can't tell me what to do,' said Shane, 'I don't have to listen to a bl—'

'Be quiet, Shane,' ordered Mr Osborne. 'I think you'd better go and change. Now.'

'I'm sorry about that,' Mr Osborne said to Chester, as Shane walked slowly off across the field. 'I can't imagine what got into the boy. Now, I'm sure you'd like to see how the rest are coming along. They're doing rather well.'

Chester started the group off on the next exercise, passing across the square and moving to a new position. Robbie found himself panicking at first, passing the ball and forgetting where to run to, but it was the same for everyone, and soon they were all laughing. Chester joined in. He seemed to be enjoying himself now, laughing with the rest of them, stroking the ball around the square. They all found themselves watching him, imitating the way he was already turning as he received the ball, ready to lay it off the next player. Robbie found it easier than any of them. He watched what Chester did, listened to what he said, and found he could do it. They stopped for a rest and Max said, grudgingly, 'You're not bad at that, are you? I can't work out what he wants me to do. I keep getting my feet in the wrong place.'

'It's dancing,' said Robbie. 'It really helps.'

'Oh, yeah?' said Max. 'Pull the other one.

Anyway, I think I'm going to stick to goal-keeping.'

By the time they finished off with a quick three-a-side game and another jog around the field Robbie was hot, tired and very happy. A fair number of mums and dads turned up to watch, and Robbie spotted his gran standing on the edge of the playground.

'What did you think then, Gran?' he said.

'I thought it all looked very professional,' said Gran. 'I'll wait for you outside and we can walk home together.'

'Why did I do that?' said Laura. 'I'm going to be so stiff, and I hardly saw him.'

'You seemed to be enjoying yourself,' said Gran, who was setting a good pace along the pavement. 'I was very impressed with that Miss MacGregor of yours. If only we'd had girls' football when I was young. I bet I'd have been brilliant.'

'Definitely,' agreed Robbie with a grin.

A low yellow car pulled up beside them. Chester leaned over. 'I just wanted a quick word with Robbie,' he said, 'if that's OK?'

'This is my gran,' said Robbie, 'and my friend, Laura.' Gran reached into the car and shook Chester's hand. Laura hung back, embarrassed.

'You did a good job with those kids,' said Gran, 'but when are we going to see you back in a United shirt? That's what I want to know. You need to pull your socks up, young man. We'll need you next week, in the Cup.'

'Gran!' said Robbie.

'You sound like a manager,' said Chester gloomily. 'That's what Ron Glover's been saying for weeks. He never dropped me before, though. He told me this morning. He says a few games in the reserves'll do me good.'

'But that's stupid.' Robbie was outraged. 'You're too good for the reserves.'

'That's what I said. He told me to go away and think about it, but I nearly got in the car and drove to London.'

'You didn't, though,' said Robbie.

'Well, I'd promised to come and help you lot, hadn't I? That's what I wanted to ask you. Was it OK? I've never done it before. I don't know what that Miss MacGregor thought.'

'It was great,' said Robbie. 'Honest! But what did you say to Mr Glover? You're not going to leave, are you?'

'No,' said Chester, 'Glover's right. I don't like admitting it, but he is. I rang him just now and said so.'

'Good lad,' said Gran. 'It happens to everyone sometime, you know. In thirty years I've seen the lot, I can tell you. You'll be back.'

'Thanks,' said Chester. 'I'll see you next week, then. And well done, Laura. You were brilliant.'

The yellow car roared off down the street and Laura blushed crimson to the roots of her hair.

CHAPTER 9

The following Tuesday, Gran drove the hundred miles to the Wanderers ground as fast as the old Mini would go.

'It's a pity Chester isn't playing,' said Robbie.

'It's a good job he isn't, if you ask me,' said Gran. 'He was as nervous as a kitten when he was doing that coaching the other night.'

'But you said it was good.'

'Well, so it was. But your teachers did most of the work. Best thing he could do, playing in reserves. Might be just what he needs. Now, let's get to this match. We're going to win. I know we are.'

Gran heaved the Mini into the fast lane and put her foot to the floor.

*　　*　　*

For a whole hour it looked as if Gran was wrong. Nothing went right for United, and Wanderers were inspired by their tiny midfield player, Dimitri Ostrakov. Just before half-time, Ostrakov twisted past two defenders and beat Alex Evans in the United goal with a delicate chip.

Things didn't improve in the second half, and United were looking like a beaten team when a Wanderers defender slipped on the edge of his own penalty area and Marty Bean slid in to level the scores. Robbie and Gran leapt up and down with the rest of the travelling supporters, but then they saw that Marty Bean was still lying injured on the ground. He was carried from the field on a stretcher.

'Young Steve Brennan's coming on,' said Gran.

'He's just a boy!' said a man behind them. 'He's a funny-looking kid!'

'He's seventeen next week,' Gran told him. She had followed Steve Brennan's career in the reserves.

'Bit risky, isn't it, throwing a kid like that into a big game like this. I wouldn't be too happy if it was my team.'

'He'll be fine,' said Gran sharply. 'He's a good lad.'

When Robbie saw the big number six who was marking Steve Brennan, he couldn't help being worried. Brennan looked so frail beside him, and his legs looked so thin. He reminded Robbie of a daddy-long-legs. Brennan was popular with the United fans and they gave him a warm welcome when he ran onto the pitch.

'He's gonna have to watch himself,' said the Wanderers fan behind them. 'He looks like he'll break into little pieces the first time Dan Ruttley tackles him!'

Robbie watched Steve Brennan closely as United began to put real pressure on Wanderers. He was amazed how far Brennan ran, especially considering he hardly touched the ball. Every time United pressed forward Brennan made a run, sometimes towards the corner flag, sometimes diagonally across the centre, sometimes checking suddenly and changing direction. Robbie found it hard to follow him; Dan Ruttley found it even harder. When the ball went out for a throw, the number six stood with his hands on his knees, gasping for breath, and that few seconds was long enough for Brennan to lose him completely. The throw was taken quickly; the defender was looking round, desperately searching for Brennan, but it was too late! Brennan took the ball to the line and whipped over a low cross, hard and fast, swinging away from the goalkeeper. Mike O'Hara volleyed the ball crisply into the net. All around, the United fans erupted. Gran leapt in the air and yelled at the top of her voice.

There were ten minutes left, and it was 2–1 to United. Wanderers pushed every player forward in an attempt to score an equalizer. To the watching United fans the last five minutes seemed to last for ever, but somehow United held out. They were through to the next round of the Cup!

In the car on the way home Robbie tried hard to keep his eyes open. He watched the white line in the middle of the road. It blurred and separated; there were two lines now and he couldn't make them go straight. Cat's-eyes glinted in the headlights. His eyes closed.

He woke up suddenly. They were driving through the outskirts of Rexford.

'All right, love. We're nearly there.'

'I had a weird dream, Gran. Chester was in it. Gran, you do think I can be a footballer, don't you? A real one, I mean.'

'You can do anything, love, if you really want to. Look at that Steve Brennan. I bet everyone told him he'd never make it!'

'Dad doesn't think so. If it was Barry practising all the time he'd probably think it was brilliant. Barry's not even all that interested in football.'

'Don't ask me to explain your dad, love. I've known him all his life and I still don't understand him. I was married to your grandad for more than thirty years and I never understood him either. You get in that team, Robbie, that's what you want, isn't it? Don't waste time worrying about what anyone else thinks.'

The day after the Wanderers game, Chester Smith returned for the second coaching session. His first game in the reserves had gone well, and he seemed a lot more cheerful. Mr Pitt's lads grumbled constantly whenever Chester was out of earshot, and in the PE lesson during the week that followed, Mr Pitt carried on as if Chester's coaching had never taken place. It was Miss Jones who put Chester's ideas into practice with the girls, as Mr Pitt looked on in disbelief.

'The woman's mad,' he said, as he

organized the lads for their match. Several boys, Robbie included, who had been doing well in the coaching sessions were abandoned as usual to the Bog.

Another week passed. United played a difficult game away from home and came out with an excellent 1–1 draw after Steve Brennan scored a late equalizer. Chester had another game in the reserves, and then he failed to turn up for the third coaching session.

'Right,' said Miss MacGregor. 'No sense waiting. We may as well start warming up. Mr Smith has no doubt been held up in the traffic. Five minutes' jogging everyone.'

As they came back round the field for the second time Robbie saw Chester's car pull into the car park, and as Chester ran from the car to the field, Robbie was sure he could see an extra bounce in his stride. When the last stragglers had returned and after Chester had finished signing autographs for the small crowd of onlookers, he took over the warm-up.

'Can we have a match today?' someone shouted.

Chester grinned. 'It's a pain, isn't it, practising all the time. You've got to do it though.' There were groans. 'Hold on,' he continued. 'You get yourselves sorted, you should get through all that stuff we did last week in half the time. Then we can have some six-a-sides.' They all cheered. 'Well, go on then. What are you waiting for? Same groups as last week. Get on with it.'

For a few moments there was chaos as they tried to find their way to last week's groups. Then, suddenly, astonishingly, everyone was busy: passing, running, controlling the ball, intercepting. Chester moved around the groups, giving advice where it was needed, but for the teachers there was very little to do. Miss MacGregor and Miss Jones watched their group of girls with a look of satisfaction on their faces.

'A lot of these kids have got talent, Miss MacGregor,' said Chester. 'You could put a good team together.'

'There *is* a competition,' Miss MacGregor told him. 'A tournament, in fact. It's next Monday, though. Do you think they could be ready in time?'

'I don't see why not,' said Chester. 'Let's see them playing a game.'

Mr Osborne handed out bibs to Robbie's group. 'Yellow team,' he said. 'Max, Jake, Jamie, Shane, David and Robbie.'

'Aw, sir,' moaned Shane, 'do we have to have him? He's rubbish.'

'Don't be ridiculous,' said Mr Osborne. 'I really am getting very tired of your attitude. You would have been banned before now if it hadn't been for Mr Smith.'

'It's all right, sir,' said Robbie, 'I don't want to be in that team anyway.'

'Now *you're* being ridiculous,' snapped Mr Osborne. 'Get those bibs on quickly. Mr Smith wants to say something.'

'You're only allowed three touches,' Chester told them. 'Two to control the ball and one to pass or shoot. You've got to think. You'll have to move around, look for space. Everyone ready? OK, then let's go!'

Robbie stood alone on the pitch. Mr Osborne was talking to Chester, and the rest of the team were in a huddle, arguing.

'I'm going to be striker,' said Shane.

'Don't be stupid,' said Jake. 'I should be. I'm much better than you.'

'Says who?'

'We're starting,' said Max, pulling on the enormous pair of goalkeeping gloves that made his hands look four times their actual size. 'If you're all going to be attackers, I'd better have Robbie in defence.'

'What's the use of that?' said Jake. 'I'll go

back. Let Shane be striker or we'll never hear the end of it.'

The Blues kicked off, and instantly one of their attackers, Ian Johnstone, was running into space in front of Robbie.

'Mark him then, Robbie,' yelled Max.

Just for a fraction of a second, Robbie was gripped by panic, then he heard Chester's voice.

'Come on, Robbie, move!'

He put everything out of his mind except sticking with Ian. He remembered the big Wanderers defender, Dan Ruttley, and how Steve Brennan had tricked him. He wasn't going to let that happen to him. Ian was good; he kept Robbie on his toes, but he couldn't get away from him.

Then at last the ball was played to Ian. His first touch was good, but Robbie's presence was enough to put him off, and with his next touch the ball bobbled away from him. Robbie cut in quickly, whipped the ball away with the outside of his foot, and looked up to see Shane yelling for it. He didn't hesitate; with his second touch he hit a crisp pass that cut between two Blue defenders right to Shane's feet. The ball was travelling fast – far faster than Shane had expected. Before he could control it, it had passed under his foot and run out of play.

Robbie heard Gran's voice. 'Good ball, Robbie! Keep it up.'

'You hit that too hard,' Shane was walking towards Robbie. 'You should have waited. I wasn't ready. If you get the ball again, you just give it to Jake, all right?'

'Concentrate, Shane,' said Mr Osborne. The Blues had taken their throw and were attacking again.

As Robbie ran back, chasing Ian, Jake yelled, 'Ignore him. It was a great pass, OK?' Robbie hardly heard him. He was putting all his energy into focusing on the game, tracking back with Ian, giving him no room at all, but a part of him knew that something had changed; that the others were at least beginning to take him seriously.

One of the Blues played a loose pass, and Jake was on to it in a flash. Suddenly the Yellows had the initiative, and Robbie had a chance to turn quickly away from Ian and call for the ball. Jake saw him sprinting into space and played a perfect pass for him to run on to. Robbie took the ball in his stride, and with his first touch pushed it beyond the defender who was rushing towards him.

He was well into the Blue half now, racing for the dead ball line. At the last possible moment he hooked it back across the goal towards the waiting Shane, who blasted it first time high over the crossbar.

'You're meant to be a defender,' Shane began. 'That cross was rubbish.' But Robbie didn't wait to listen. He was already trotting back into position, marking Ian again. Mr Osborne blew for half-time.

Before the game could restart, Chester came over.

'I'd like to see what some of you do in different positions,' he said. He re-organized the Blues, then turned to the Yellows.

'Jake, I'd like to see you up front. Then Robbie and . . . David is it? You two in midfield. Shane and Jamie at the back. You look like you're happy in goal,' he said to Max.

Shane gave Chester an angry look, but said nothing. Robbie looked around to see what else was happening. On the next pitch Miss MacGregor's team of girls was playing a boys' team. Barry was in goal, and he didn't look happy. The girls seemed to be doing well. He watched Laura control the ball and play a good pass, then it was time to start again.

With the new organization things were very different. The moment Robbie touched the ball he felt something special was happening. He flicked it to David, who played it almost instantly to Jake. Jake laid the ball back to Robbie again. Robbie saw the run that Jake was making and slid the ball past the last defender as Jake ran on to it. He slotted it calmly into the net. Gran yelled with excitement, and Robbie heard her shout, 'Well done, Robbie!'; but it was the smile on Jake's face that mattered most to him.

Robbie felt as if he was floating on air. Everything he tried came off; all his flicks and touches found his own players. In defence there was nothing for Shane to do, and gradually he crept further and further forward. Robbie had the ball again and Shane, taking him by surprise, shoved him out of the way. Mr Osborne started to blow his whistle, then stopped, confused. Shane pushed the ball forward, and raced after it, preparing to shoot, but he had pushed it too far, and one of the Blues stepped forward to control the ball. Shane didn't pause. Robbie heard Jake shouting, 'Shane, *stop*!' Shane's foot was already flying through the air as the Blue player passed the ball. Shane's boot scythed his legs from under him and the player hit the ground with a thump.

Mr Osborne blew his whistle, and Chester ran on to the field.

'What do you think you're doing, you stupid . . . ?'

'It's all right, Mr Smith,' said Mr Osborne. 'We don't tolerate that kind of thing here. That was extremely dangerous, young man. You . . .'

'Stuff you!' said Shane. 'You don't know what you're talking about. I wouldn't play in your stupid team if you paid me.'

'You tell 'em, Shazza,' came a voice from the touchline. Robbie looked up. It was Shane's brother, Darren, with a couple of his mates. Mr Osborne walked over and spoke to them as Shane went off to the changing room, but they turned away from him and walked out of the gate, jeering and swearing as they went.

CHAPTER 10

Mr Pitt was walking towards his car when he heard the ripple of applause from the field. He'd told Miss MacGregor he couldn't help because he had too much work to do, but he wasn't sure she'd believed him. He walked to the edge of the playground, and even he could see that there was a lot of very impressive football being played. In spite of himself he edged nearer, and when the games ended, he found that he was a lot closer to Miss MacGregor than he had intended.

'Well now, Mr Pitt,' she called, her eyes glittering with excitement, 'this is quite something, isn't it? You'll be amazed to learn that my team of girls have actually beaten a team of boys.'

'Huh!' snorted Mr Pitt. 'This isn't football. Football's a contact sport. A lot of these kids would fall apart if they had to face up to a real tackle, especially the girls.'

'I don't think so,' said Chester, coming over to join them, 'but you'll see soon enough. I think we should definitely enter this competition.'

'What competition?'

'Mr Smith thinks we might enter the Inter-School tournament, Mr Pitt. He's offered to give up a great deal of his spare time to help us.'

'I pick the team,' said Mr Pitt. 'I told you.'

'And I'm telling you, Mr Pitt, that Chester Smith is in charge of the team, and it will be selected from those children who are here this afternoon. If you came back simply to make trouble I think it would be best if you leave now. I'll see you in my office in the morning.'

Wayne Straker of the *Daily Comet* rounded up Nigel Finch, his photographer, who was busy taking pictures of Robbie and his gran. The afternoon had been a total washout as far as Straker was concerned.

'Do me a favour, son,' Straker grumbled as he dragged Finch away. 'An old woman and a kid. That ain't news. We're out of here!'

'What about the story?' asked Chester. 'We had a deal, remember.'

'We'll manage something. You got your snaps, Nigel? I mean, it's not exactly earth-shattering stuff is it, Chester? Not your front-page material.'

'I thought it was pretty good actually, Wayne,' said Finch. 'I mean, Chester did an awfully good job. I've got some terrific shots.'

'You tell him!' said Gran. 'About time we had something cheerful to read about on the sports pages if you ask me.'

'I couldn't agree more, madam,' said Mr Osborne, a little out of breath. He looked, thought Robbie, a lot younger after running around.

'This is my gran, sir,' said Robbie. 'She's been a United fan all her life.'

'Pleased to meet you, ma'am.' Mr Osborne bowed slightly as he shook Gran's hand. 'You have a talented grandson.' He pulled on his dusty old jacket and seemed to shrink in front of their eyes. 'Yes, well, I must be off. Books to mark, timetables to arrange.'

Mr Osborne scuttled away across the play-ground.

'You just came here looking for dirt,' said Chester to Straker. 'We had a deal you were going to write something good.'

'All right! All right! You'll get your piece. Chester Smith helps the little kiddies. Just like you wanted. But if you don't mind we've got a pile-up on the motorway to cover. See you later.'

Miss MacGregor called them together at the end of the session.

'When you're changed,' she said, 'I'd like you in the gym for five minutes. There's a six-a-side competition next week and we're entering two teams.'

Robbie found his hands trembling as he changed. He could hardly do up his buttons. He knew he'd played well but, even so, most of the others were older than him, and bigger. He kept thinking about what the reporter had said, about Chester just doing it to make himself look good. It wasn't like that – was it?

The rest of them were all arguing about who would be in the team. Barry's voice was raised above the others.

'You can't tell from those games. It's going

to be a competition, isn't it? They'll want people who are strong. There won't be any of this two-touch rubbish. You'll need defenders who can stop people.'

Max came and sat down beside Robbie. 'Is he like that all the time?' he asked, nodding towards Barry.

'Most of it,' said Robbie. 'He can be all right though, if you get him away from Shane for long enough.'

'He won't like it when you're in the team, then.'

'But he's right, though, isn't he? Everyone else is older. Or bigger.'

'Oh, come off it. You were brilliant. Anyone could see, even your big brother. I saw him watching you. If he hadn't been doing that, he wouldn't have let so many goals in. He's jealous. But I wanted to ask you – do you really think dancing helps you play football?'

'That's what Chester said.'

'D'you think it . . . you know . . . would work for goalkeepers?'

Robbie looked at him and grinned.

'Bound to,' he said.

'OK,' said Miss MacGregor, 'you've all worked very hard, but I'm afraid we can only enter two teams for the competition.'

'Is there a girls' team, Miss MacGregor?' asked Laura.

'I'm afraid not.'

'But that's not fair,' said Laura. 'We beat the boys.'

'Well, I'm not entirely sure you should have been playing against them at all,' said Miss MacGregor, smiling. 'We'll have to see what we can arrange in the future. Now, the teams. The 'A' team is Max Jenkins in goal, Martin Black, Nicky Slater, Jake Potter, Robbie Devlin and Ian Johnstone.'

Robbie didn't even hear the 'B' team being announced. He kept saying to himself, over and over, *I'm in the team . . . I'm in the team . . .* He started to picture how he was going to walk in through the door at home as if nothing had happened, and say, 'Oh, by the way, Dad . . .'

'Come on, Robbie,' Gran tapped him on the shoulder.

'One moment,' called Miss MacGregor. 'I'm sure you'd all like to know before you go. I wanted Mr Smith to tell you, but he seems to have lost his tongue. He tells me he's back in his First Team squad. Apparently he scored an excellent goal for the reserves on Wednesday. Congratulations, Mr Smith!'

Everyone cheered, and Chester looked as if he wished he was somewhere else.

'That's great,' said Robbie as they walked out of the gate. 'We'll see him play on Saturday.'

'Barry!' Gran called out. 'Where are you off to? Walk home with us.'

Barry was not in either team. Neither was Shane. Barry hadn't expected to be in the team. In fact, Barry didn't really care that much about football, but Shane did, and Shane was his mate. Barry could see Robbie was good; of course he could, anyone could – but that didn't make it any easier.

Robbie saw Barry standing there, hesitating, then he heard Shane's voice, calling from the corner. There was a gang of them there, big kids mostly.

'I'll see you later,' said Barry.

'Where's Barry?' Mum asked, as she put Robbie's tea on the table.

'He's off with his stupid mates,' Robbie said. 'Don't you want to know what happened? At football training?'

'Sorry, love. I was worried about him, that's all. He hasn't been himself lately. Anyway, I don't need to ask, do I? You look like the cat that got the cream.'

'What's that?' said Dad as he sat down. 'Where's Barry?'

'I'm in the football team, Dad. We're playing on Monday night, after school, in a tournament.'

'Oh, yeah? Pull the other one, Robbie. Where *is* Barry? That's the third time this week he's been late for tea.' Dad tucked into his egg and chips.

Robbie couldn't stand it. 'I knew you wouldn't believe me,' he said. 'What do I have to do, Dad? . . . Dad?'

Dad put down his knife and fork. He stared at Robbie.

'Aren't you going to congratulate him, then?' said Mum.

Before Dad could say anything the front door opened and shut. Footsteps went up the stairs.

'Barry!' Mum called out. 'Where have you been? Your tea's getting cold.'

'I'm not hungry.' The door of Barry's room closed.

'Leave him alone,' said Dad. 'They get moody, boys that age. He'll be OK in the morning.' Mum looked doubtful, but she was already late for her evening class.

Later on, Robbie tried to talk to Barry through his door, but all he could hear was the sound of aliens being zapped on Barry's computer.

'Barry! I can't help it you didn't get in the team. It's not my fault, is it? Why d'you have to keep going round with Shane? Darren's weird.'

'Leave me alone,' said Barry. 'Of course it's your fault, all of it. Everything was all right till you started playing football.'

CHAPTER 11

Chester managed to fit in an extra coaching session that week, working mainly with the teams. They worked hard, preparing for the tournament, the two teams playing against each other until they were all exhausted. When Robbie walked into the changing room after the session he heard someone say his name, and stopped. They were talking about him. He waited outside the door, not wanting to hear, but unable to stop himself listening.

'I know he's good,' Ian was saying, 'but what if he freezes up? You saw him do it, that first time. And he's never played for a team before, has he?'

'He's OK,' Max retorted. 'Mr Pitt didn't

give him a chance, that's all.'

'What does it matter?' said Jake. 'We'll find out soon enough.'

They started talking about Chester then, and Robbie slipped in unnoticed to get changed. He wished he hadn't heard them. It hadn't occurred to him they might have any doubts about him, and now, he began to have doubts about himself . . .

On Saturday morning Robbie grabbed the *Daily Comet* out of the hands of the paper boy and scanned the back page impatiently; then he turned to the inside pages. He was still hoping for a report about the coaching; he'd been looking every day and there hadn't been a thing. Finally he saw it, tucked away at the bottom, a few measly lines.

'*Still no place in United's team for out-of-form Chester Smith. The goal he scored for the reserves this week wasn't enough to get him a place in today's starting line-up, and he's expected to be on the bench. Smith hasn't played for United since the incident earlier this month when he turned on a group of fans. Our intrepid reporters caught up with him this week helping out schoolkids with their football training.*

Very public spirited, Chester!'

'Is that it?' he said, disappointed.

'Is what it?' asked Dad. 'That's my paper. Hand it over.'

'They were supposed to write about the football training. That's it, down the bottom there. They took loads of pictures. Why didn't they put them in?'

'They probably thought nobody would be interested,' Dad answered as he poured cornflakes into a bowl.

'Bob!' Mum snapped. 'Shut up! Don't worry, Robbie. They had a bigger story, that's all. They sometimes save these things up, put them in later. Anyway, you've got the tournament to look forward to, haven't you. How's the training going?'

'Good,' said Robbie with a confidence he didn't feel. 'Chester thinks we've got a great chance.'

Dad snorted, sending a shower of half-eaten cornflakes back into his bowl. 'It's Chester now, is it? Very cosy!'

Mum shot him another look. 'I'm surprised you've stopped going, Barry. You've always been so keen on football.'

'I'm not bothered. I've better things to do.'

'Like hanging round with Shane and his big brother,' said Robbie.

'I didn't know Darren was home,' said Dad. 'You stay away from him, Barry.'

'He's Shane's brother. He's around, that's all. I can't help it.'

'He's a bit old for you, isn't he, love?' said Mum. 'Why don't you go to the football sessions, you and Shane? Gran said it was terrific last night.'

'Yeah, well we're not, all right?' Barry pushed his chair back and went upstairs.

'See!' said Dad. 'You mention football in this house, and before you know it you've got an argument. Barry doesn't have to play if he doesn't want to.'

'Well, *I'm* going to watch Robbie play on Monday,' said Mum. 'Why don't you come, Bob?'

'I don't know. I'd have to take time off work.' He caught Mum's eye. 'Look, I'll do my best, all right? I'm not promising anything though.'

Gran always came to lunch on the Saturdays when United played at home. This Saturday she arrived early.

'I've a spare ticket,' she said. 'D'you think Laura would like to come? If she can't, we could take you, Barry. What are you up to this afternoon?'

'Nothing,' Barry mumbled. Robbie ran to the phone and Barry went upstairs.

'She'll be here in ten minutes,' said Robbie, when he returned. 'Thanks, Gran.'

He stopped when he felt the silence in the room. Dad turned and went out.

'What did you say to him, Gran? You said something didn't you?'

'Never you mind, young man. Come on, let's watch *Football Focus*.'

Mum was furious when she arrived home and Dad hadn't put the potatoes on. When they finally left for the match there was no time to spare. After the great win at Wanderers there was a new air of excitement among United fans. The streets around the ground were a sea of green and white. Policemen on horses seemed to float above the crowds.

'I've never seen so many people in one place!' Laura exclaimed. There were long queues at the turnstiles, and moments after they had clanked their way through, they heard the crowd roar as the teams ran onto the pitch.

'Quick!' said Gran, as Robbie stopped to buy a programme. 'We don't want to miss the kick-off.'

Everywhere, people were rushing to find their seats. The noise of the crowd came to them distantly now, as they hurried beneath the high wall of the South Stand, passing flights of steps leading upwards into the dark openings at the top. As they passed each opening, the roar hit them, as if a wild beast was caged there.

'Here we are,' said Gran, 'block J. I've been sitting in this block at every home game for the last thirty years.'

'Every game!' gasped Laura, struggling to keep pace with Gran as she ran up the steps.

'That's right. Never miss a match, do I, Sid?' She fired this question at the wizened, white-coated steward who was guarding the entrance to the stand.

'Afternoon, Mrs Devlin. She's never missed a game to my knowledge,' he said to Laura, 'but you'll miss this one if you don't get a move on.'

'Wow!' exclaimed Laura. It was dark here at the top of the stand, where the roof came down sharply to meet the wall behind them. The rows of seats dropped away beneath them: a seething mountainside of green and white. And there, shining brilliant emerald, was the pitch. The winter afternoon was

111

dark, and the floodlights were already on. They walked quickly down the steps, and when Gran stopped, a dozen rows from the front, Laura found that the players, who had seemed small and far away from the top, now seemed larger than life, like brightly lit actors on a stage.

'You can hear them shouting to each other,' she said. 'You never hear them shouting on the telly.'

'I thought you never watched football,' said Robbie.

'Come along,' said Gran. 'Here we are, Row L. Our seats are just along there.'

'There's Chester!' Robbie pointed, excited. 'And Steve Brennan. They're out there, warming up.'

'Steve Brennan's in the team,' said Laura, 'but Chester's a substitute; it says here in the programme.'

'Glover won't play Smith if he doesn't have to,' said the man next to them. 'I reckon he's gone off him after what happened. Can't wait to be rid of him, if you ask me.'

'I didn't,' said Robbie angrily. He stood on his seat, and yelled at the top of his voice. 'Chester!'

Chester looked up and saw him. He

grinned and waved, then turned to sit on the bench. As he did so Robbie heard shouting and grumbling a few rows in front. There were people pushing their way into a group of empty seats near the touchline, swearing loudly at spectators who didn't get out of their way fast enough. Then the whistle blew and the game began.

It was an unfamiliar United team that lined up on the pitch. Ron Glover had obviously decided to bring on some of his younger players from the reserves. Three of them had never played for the first team before. Des Wall and Simon Craddock were playing together at the centre of the United defence. They were both big, but even to Robbie they looked very young, and extremely nervous. Right from the start United were under pressure, and time after time the other defenders, Nigel Shelfe and Pete Lock had to make vital interceptions to get the younger players out of trouble.

High above the ground in a glass cage sat the radio commentary team.

'I have to say, Kenny,' said Alvin Brown during a lull in play, 'I don't think I've seen a worse performance this season.' The second half had begun, and United were trailing 2–0. 'None of the United players know what they're supposed to be doing. They look lost! What do you make of it, Kenny?'

'They've lost their shape completely, Alvin. Glover obviously believes in these youngsters, but it's all looking a bit much for them at the moment.'

'You're right there. And I don't know about you, Kenny, but I don't think O'Hara's match-fit. Wait a second. Young Brennan's picked up the ball, deep in the United half of the field, the best of these young United players. This is better from United. He's got some movement in front of him now, plays a marvellous pass to O'Hara and . . . *ohhhhhh!* O'Hara's gone down. Did you see what happened there, Kenny? It looked to me as if he just gave up! Now we've got the physio on the pitch . . . he's waving to Ron Glover on the touchline, saying he wants a stretcher.'

'I think it must be this flu that's been going around, Alvin.'

'You may be right, Kenny. It looks like Chester Smith's coming on.'

Down on the bench, Glover looked at Chester. Both the other subs were defenders, even less experienced than the two who were having such a nightmare already.

'Right,' he said. 'This is your chance, lad. I was only going to give you the last twenty minutes, ease you back in gently, but I've no choice. Get yourself warmed up quick.'

As Chester stood on the touchline, a roar began to grow in the crowd – a roar with words, echoing around the stadium: '*One Chester Smith, there's only one Chester Smith . . .*' He let the sound of it fill his mind. He smelt the grass, felt the blaze of the floodlights, felt a great surge of energy run through him like electricity as he ran onto the pitch. Pete Lock, the captain, had placed the ball for the free kick. Chester ran up to him.

'Do you want to look like a no-hoper on *Match of the Day* tonight?' he laughed. 'Or shall we get on and win this game?'

Pete Lock looked at Chester, saw the confidence that had returned to his face, and slapped his outstretched hand.

'You're on!' he said. 'Now get out of my way while I score.'

'I think Smith wants to take it,' said Alvin Brown. 'He's saying something to Lock. Looks like some kind of a signal. Smith's running into the box. Lock's going to take it. Oh my word! What a strike! That fairly scorched into the net. Unbelievable! And totally against the run of play. That's brought the crowd to their feet. Maybe Smith's going to bring them luck. He's fished the ball out of the back of the net. Look at that. He wants to get on with the game. He's run all the way to the centre spot and placed the ball . . . now City kick off . . . Maddle to Johnson, midway inside the United half now . . . over by the far touch-line . . . and there's Brennan challenging for the ball . . . first time we've seen anything from him, Kenny.'

'That's right, Alvin. He's come out of that inside right channel and he looks hungry for the ball . . .'

'Brennan moves forward . . . Smith's made a marvellous run down below us . . . I don't know if Brennan has spotted him . . . Yes! . . . He has! . . . He's hit a wonderful crossfield ball. Inch perfect. Must be all of fifty yards . . . Now Smith's on the ball . . . But hold on . . . there's some kind of disturbance down there . . . Smith's stopped . . . I can't quite see what's going on.'

Robbie watched Chester control the ball. It was beautiful, effortless. Then he heard the yells, just a few rows in front. People were on their feet, chanting, screaming

116

insults at Chester, making monkey noises. A couple of bananas flew from the crowd. Robbie willed Chester to ignore them, and he did. He looked up, ready to hit his pass, but then Robbie saw him clap a hand to his head. Something small and round had hit him, and he stopped, hesitated just for a moment, just long enough for his marker to nick the ball away from him and set up a new City attack. There was a groan from the crowd.

Chester bent down and picked up the object that had hit him. He'd ignored the bananas and the insults, but he couldn't ignore the stinging pain above his ear. He looked at the shiny fifty-pence piece, and he called the referee over. The ref took the coin to a policeman standing by the side of the pitch.

'Be fair!' said the policeman. 'How can we tell who chucked that out of a crowd this size?'

'Well you have it announced over the public address system,' said the ref. 'Any more objects and I'm stopping the game.'

Suddenly Robbie realized that Gran was gone, her seat empty. There she was, in the gangway, waving her umbrella.

'Gran, come back!' he yelled, stumbling

over people's legs with Laura in his wake. 'Where are you going?'

Gran turned. Her eyes were burning. 'I'm sick to death of these thugs,' she said. 'I'm going down there to get a policeman and have them arrested. And if the police won't arrest them I'll sort them out myself!'

CHAPTER 12

Gran stuck out her chin, and marched down to the foot of the gangway.

'Constable! Constable! Come here, please! Over here!' The policeman had just finished talking to the referee. He half turned. He didn't want to miss any of the action. United were about to take a throw-in. 'Yes, madam?'

'Are you going to do something about those . . . those . . . animals up there, or am I going to have to do it myself?'

The policeman sighed, and walked nearer. 'What seems to be the trouble, madam?'

'Are you deaf? Are you blind? Can't you hear what they're shouting? And they're throwing things. There has to be a law against it. Go and arrest them!' The policeman looked up at the row of hate-filled faces, some of them standing and shaking their fists. Robbie looked too.

'Gran! That's Shane Peabody! And his brother, Darren. And—' He stopped suddenly, not quite sure of what he'd seen, just a glimpse of a pale, worried face. Then Shane stood up and shook his fist, and there was no doubt any more. Behind Shane, next to Darren, Robbie saw Barry.

'Well?' demanded Gran. 'What are you going to do?' There was a groan from the crowd as another United move broke down.

The policeman hesitated. 'I'm not sure there's anything I can do, madam,' he said. 'Why don't you just go back to your seat and enjoy the match. They're a little over-excited, but they're not doing any real harm.'

'You're afraid of them!' said Gran, her eyes flashing. 'I know there's some kind of a law against what they're doing, and even if there wasn't, anyone with a scrap of decency would want them stopped. You're a disgrace to your uniform, young man! I'll just have to put a stop to this myself!' She turned and marched back up the gangway.

'Gran!' cried Robbie. 'Gran, don't, please don't, you'll get hurt.'

'Bah!' said Gran. 'Even beasts like them wouldn't dare hurt a woman. I'll give them what for!'

Robbie turned to Laura. 'You'll have to get help. There's another policeman along there. Quick!' Laura dashed off along the foot of the stand.

Waving her umbrella in front of her like a sword, Gran marched along the row of seats.

'Get up, get up!' she yelled at the people in the seats. 'If you don't want to help me, get out of my way.' She stared up at the boy standing next to Darren. He was wearing a white vest with a Union Jack drawn on it in felt-tip pen. His face was twisted with hate as he yelled abuse at Chester, now far away in the centre of the pitch. He didn't notice Gran until she poked him in the stomach with the tip of her umbrella. The people in the nearby seats were standing up.

'You want something, old woman?' he sneered. 'You got a problem?'

'No,' retorted Gran. '*You've* got a problem. I'm making a citizen's arrest. What you've been doing, it's against the law, and I'm staying here till the police come to take you away.'

'Oh yeah! You and whose army? Look at this lot. They don't care. I bet they don't like blacks any more than we do. Why don't you sit down? You're blocking my view.'

Gran brandished her umbrella again, and the boy grabbed hold of it. There was a brief struggle and the boy shoved Gran away from him.

'Gran!' yelled Robbie. 'Look out!'

Everything seemed to happen in slow-motion. Gran toppled over the row of seats behind her, but at the very last moment a man dived forward and threw himself beneath her as she fell. Gran's head glanced off the side of a seat. All around them the eyes of the spectators had turned from the pitch to what was happening in the crowd, and an angry murmur began to spread. Robbie pushed people out of the way to get to Gran, who was struggling back to her feet. There was an ugly graze above her right eye, but she was still ready for battle.

'Gran, don't!' Robbie shouted. Some of the other spectators rushed to Gran and grabbed her arms.

'Come on, Mrs Devlin,' said one of them, looking pale and angry. 'I'm sure the police will be here in a moment. You're not going to do any good by getting yourself hurt.'

'Get your hands off me!' Gran struggled to free herself. Then a surprised expression passed across her face and she sank back into the man's arms.

'Gran!' Robbie gasped, close to tears. 'Gran, you are all right, aren't you? Say you're all right!'

Gran smiled weakly at Robbie. Other spectators placed coats along the seats and they laid Gran down. The game was still going on, but for the moment no-one nearby had eyes for anyone but Gran. Above them the gang who had been chanting so loudly were sitting in an unnatural silence and stirring uneasily in their seats. They were prevented from leaving by a solid wall of grim-faced spectators. Robbie looked for Barry, and saw that Darren Peabody had a tight grip on his arm. Barry's eyes were pleading with Robbie to do something, but there was nothing he *could* do. He could see that Barry had got himself into something he couldn't get out of. He prayed Gran wouldn't catch sight of him. That would be too much.

'Move aside there. Come along. Police! Make way!'

The crowd split apart and a police inspector appeared, followed by more policemen and stewards, and finally by Laura.

'He attacked that old lady!'

'I wasn't doing any harm,' mumbled the boy. 'Minding my own business I was and she comes along and assaults me. You going to arrest her then?'

'Just hold on a minute please, everyone,' said the inspector. He hopped over the backs of the seats to where Gran was lying, and looked at her face.

'Is this right, madam? One of these lads assaulted you?' Gran nodded. 'Can you point him out to me?'

'In the middle,' said Gran. 'With the Union Jack on his vest.'

'Right,' said the inspector. 'There seems to be no shortage of witnesses. I shall need a statement from you, madam, but I think the first thing to do is to make sure you're checked over by a doctor. Send down for a stretcher,' he said to one of the men behind him. Gran tried to sit up.

'Now, now!' said the inspector. 'You've had a nasty shock. Just you lie there quietly till the doctor arrives. Meanwhile we shall have the rest of these troublemakers ejected from the ground as quickly as possible.'

'You should have done that in the first place,' said Gran. 'And I'm feeling much better now,' she added, sitting up and looking around. Stewards were leading the gang away. Robbie saw the back of Barry's head as he was led off along the side of the pitch. He still couldn't believe it.

People crowded round, all trying to tell Gran how wonderful she was.

'Please,' said the inspector, 'if you could all return to your seats. Ah, good, here comes the stretcher,'

'But I'll miss the match!' Gran exclaimed. 'I've never missed a match! I'm fine. Just let me go and sit down.'

'I'm afraid I must insist that you're checked over, madam. I'm sure that if you are OK, they'll arrange for you to watch the rest of the game in comfort. Come along now, onto the stretcher.'

'Please, Gran,' pleaded Robbie. 'You're still shaking.' Gran looked at Robbie's worried face, and sat on the stretcher. 'We can come too, can't we?' Robbie said to the two women from St John's Ambulance who were carrying the stretcher.

'Sure,' they replied. 'Just follow along behind us.'

Robbie and Laura followed the stretcher down the gangway and through a gate out on the cinder track at the edge of the pitch.

CHAPTER 13

With a shock, Robbie realized that the game was still going on. The City winger was only inches away from him. He could have reached out and touched him. For the moment, thoughts of Barry were driven out of his mind.

City had a corner at the far end. Robbie saw the ball float into the area, and the big City centre-half rise towards it; then Chester rose even higher and headed the ball clear. 'Stop!' he begged. 'Let's just watch this! Please.' The ambulance-women looked at each other, and at Gran. They stopped, and Gran raised herself on one elbow to watch.

As Chester ran back for the corner, he

saw the stewards leading a group of fans away. One of them turned and shook his fist at Chester, before the steward took a firmer hold on his arm. At last! Chester thought, maybe this is going to work out after all!

He was marking the big City defender, Gus Salmon, who always went forward for corners. Chester had played against him many times. He knew that Salmon would hold back until the last moment, relax as if he wasn't going to bother to go for the ball, and then sprint suddenly forward. He'd scored a lot of goals like that, and United simply couldn't afford to let in another one. When Salmon made his run, Chester was ready for him, timed his jump to perfection and headed the ball clear, right into the path of Kenny Tuttle. Tuttle had loads of space. City had thrown men forward for the corner, hoping to kill off the game.

'Take it, Kenny!' yelled Chester. 'Come on! Get forward!' He was already moving himself, and away to his left he could see Steve racing down the touchline with his marker ten yards behind him and losing ground.

'Yes!!' Chester shouted. 'Give it to Steve. Now!'

Kenny Tuttle looked up and saw Steve

flying ahead of him. Another second and he'd be over the halfway line, and offside. Kenny passed, a long ball curving perfectly into the vast empty spaces on the City half of the field. The crowd were roaring them forward. City players were trying desperately to get back as Steve took the ball towards the left-hand corner of the City penalty area. Chester was racing towards the goal, neck and neck with Salmon. He could see Steve preparing to cross the ball. He felt the back of his neck tingling. He knew what Steve was going to do. Chester pretended to stumble, and Salmon tried to stop with him. As Steve played the ball, Chester shot forward with a sudden, astonishing turn of speed, and volleyed it past the goalkeeper. The crowd erupted. Chester ran to Steve and lifted him into the air, and then they were both buried by a heap of United players.

When Chester stood up again, he felt as if a great weight had been lifted off his shoulders. The crowd were chanting his name again. Applause crackled in the air like electricity. He ran back, and the whistle blew. The roar of the crowd grew to a crescendo again.

'What do you think?' Robbie asked Laura,

but Laura was too ecstatic to reply, and she had eyes and ears only for what was happening on the pitch.

'City kick-off,' said Alvin Brown. 'And now they know they're in a match. What a turnaround.'

'I'll say! United have hold of the ball again, a great tackle from young Wall to win the ball from Mullet. He looks a different player now. You can almost see the confidence flowing through this United side. Wall to Craddock, to Shelfe. Now Tuttle brings it forward. Slips it sideways to Lock. Nice, fluent passing movement from United. Now it's out to Crunch, wide on the right. Crosses early, hard, to the near post. Smith flicks it on. Ohhhhh! And Tuttle came flying in there, but he just couldn't make it! Ran the whole length of the pitch, Kenny, to get on the end of that one.'

'That's right, Alvin!'

'Goal kick to City. Nigel Place takes his time over this one. I think City would be glad to hang in there for the draw. United players are complaining to the referee. They think they can win this. Here comes the kick. Crunch heads it back in towards the City goal. Oh, and that's a marvellous piece of skill from Smith. Just a casual little flick to put Brennan away in acres of space. Brennan beats a defender. He's pushed it too far, has he? No! He keeps it in. Looks up. Pulls the ball back to Smith on the edge of the area. And Smith chips the keeper. It's going in! It's a goal! Magnificent! I don't know if you can still hear us over all this noise. Watch that on *Match of the Day* tonight. That has to be one of the best goals of the season. I think we can safely say that Chester Smith is back! Kenny?'

'Great goal, Alvin. Marvellous play by young Steve Brennan down the left. They've got a great understanding those two!'

The final whistle blew. All round the ground the crowd rose to their feet, clapping, shouting, cheering. Just about the only person in the whole ground still sitting down was Gran.

The doctor had pronounced her fit enough to watch the rest of the game. 'Tough as old boots!' he said. A steward had taken them to the side of the pitch where the disabled spectators watched from their wheelchairs and found them some folding seats. They had a wonderful view of the winning goal, and Gran had leapt to her feet, cheering at the top of her voice. Now that the match was over, she suddenly felt as weak as a kitten. Everything seemed to be swimming in front of her eyes.

'Gran?' said Robbie, worried. 'What's the matter?'

'Nothing's the matter,' said Gran. 'We won, didn't we?'

She smiled happily, and passed out.

CHAPTER 14

Mum looked up from her books when she heard the front door open. Dad was down at the allotment and she was enjoying the Saturday afternoon on her own.

'Barry? Is that you?'

The kitchen door opened and she saw Barry's face.

'Barry? What's the matter? What's happened?'

There was a silence. Then Barry said, 'It wasn't my fault. I couldn't stop them.'

'For heaven's sake, Barry. You're not making sense.'

'It's Gran,' said Barry. 'At the match. She got hurt.'

'What match? You didn't go to the match.

You never go. What do you mean, Gran's hurt? Where is she?'

'It's OK. She's all right . . . at least I think so.'

'It's obviously *not* OK,' said Mum. 'I think you'd better start at the beginning.'

Bit by bit Mum dragged it out of him: how Shane and Darren had said they could go to the match and see Chester Smith make a fool of himself, how it didn't seem such a bad idea until he saw what Darren and his mates were doing. He told Mum how Gran had tried to stop them, and what had happened next. When a grim-faced Mum had fetched Dad from the allotment he repeated it all for Dad.

'What?' shouted Dad. 'What on earth have you been doing, Barry? Where's Mum now? What do you mean, someone shoved her?'

'In the face,' said Barry. 'It was horrible. She just kind of fell over backwards, and they all laughed.'

'But where is she now? What happened to her? Is she all right? For God's sake, Barry, what do you think you were doing?'

'I told you,' said Barry, 'I didn't know they were going to be like that. It was just a bit of fun. It's your fault anyway.

You always said he was rubbish.'

'My fault? My fault! I asked you a question, Barry. Where's Gran?'

'She's OK. Last time I saw her she was sitting by the side of the pitch, watching the match.'

The phone rang in the hall, and Mum went to answer it. 'They've taken her to hospital,' she called out after a minute or two. 'They say there's nothing to worry about, they just want to check her over. Robbie's gone with her.'

'She's mad!' said Dad. 'What did she think she was doing?'

'Shut up, Bob!' said Mum. 'If you can't say anything sensible, don't say anything at all. I'm going to the hospital. You can stay here with Barry. If he hadn't had to listen to the rubbish you come out with sometimes he'd probably never have got involved. Perhaps you can talk some sense into each other.'

'How is she?' said Mum.

'OK, I think,' Robbie replied.

Gran was comfortably installed in her hospital bed. She had plenty of people fussing around her and Robbie had felt in the way. He'd been waiting outside the ward, worrying.

'Mum,' he said, hesitantly, 'have you seen Barry?'

'I certainly have. He told me everything. He's at home now, with Dad. I should think that was the last straw for your gran, seeing him there with those . . . those . . .'

'But she didn't, Mum. She never saw him. I'm sure. And he didn't know they were going to do that. I know he didn't.'

'I don't know about that,' said Mum. 'Let's just make sure Gran doesn't find out tonight. She'll have to know some time, but not now.'

'Where's Bob, then?' said Gran, trying to lever herself into a sitting position. 'And Barry? Where's Barry? You'd think Bob would come and see his own mother in her hospital bed. He's just like his dad. I bet he's fiddling about in that greenhouse of his.'

'Lie down,' said Mum. 'You won't do yourself any good getting worked up. We didn't want to tire you out with too many visitors, that's all.'

'I wish people wouldn't keep telling me to lie down. Young woman! Over here! Tell them there's nothing wrong with me!' A doctor was walking towards them.

'I'm pretty sure that all Mrs Devlin needs

is a good night's rest,' said the doctor, smiling. 'But we're keeping her in overnight, just to be on the safe side. And now,' she went on, 'I think you should all be going, so we can let Mrs Devlin get some sleep.'

'You must be joking! I'm not going to sleep yet,' said Gran. 'I'm watching *Match of the Day*. I might be on it!'

'That's right!' said the lady in the next bed, who had a large white bandage covering most of her head. 'We all want to watch it, don't we?'

'Yeah!'

'Wouldn't miss it for anything!' said the people in the other beds.

'Oh, well,' said the doctor, 'so long as it's not keeping anyone awake who wants to be asleep, and so long as Sister doesn't object . . .'

'I'd like to see her stop me!' said Gran.

At that moment, they heard Sister's voice in the corridor behind them. 'I'm very sorry, but visiting time ended over an hour ago. There are people in there trying to rest, and I can't have them disturbed . . . I don't care who you are, I'm not having my patients disturbed at this time of night.'

'It's Chester!' said Robbie. 'Nobody minds

if Chester Smith comes in to see Gran, do they?' A ripple of excitement ran round the ward. Robbie pushed open the swing doors and found Sister, with her hands on her hips, blocking the entrance while Chester pleaded with her. He was almost hidden by an enormous bunch of flowers. Steve Brennan was with him. They looked like two little boys being ticked off by a policeman.

'Please, Sister,' said Robbie. 'It's not just Gran. Everyone wants to meet him.'

'I'm in charge of this ward,' said Sister, 'and I have the welfare of my patients to think about. They need their sleep. I'll take Mrs Devlin the flowers, but I really must insist that you leave now.'

'But you said they could watch *Match of the Day*, didn't you?'

'I said no such thing!'

'Sorry!' The doctor poked her head out of the office. 'I was just about to mention it to Sister when these two appeared. I was waiting for the right moment.'

'Mention what?' said Sister.

'Well, I did say Mrs Devlin could watch *Match of the Day* . . . if you have no objection that is?'

The swing doors opened a crack and a

bandaged head poked through.

'It *is* him!'

'Hold on!' came a voice from the ward. 'I want to see!'

'And me!'

'Just pass me those crutches, will you, love?'

'Stop!' cried Sister, as the bandaged lady thrust a clipboard at Chester, saying, 'I couldn't have your autograph, could I, Chester, for my little boy?'

Chester reached for the clipboard, but Sister pounced. 'Really, Mrs White, these are your notes! Has everyone gone mad? This is a hospital and it's nearly half past nine. You should all . . .'

'Half past nine!' said Mrs White. 'Quick! The telly! We'll miss it!'

Sister thew her hands in the air, then fell back into a chair. Chester and Steve tiptoed past her into the ward.

'Don't worry, Sister,' said the doctor. 'I'll stay and keep an eye on things. Make sure nobody gets over-excited.'

Gary Lineker's face filled the screen. 'I don't think much of that jacket!' said Gran. 'I thought the one he had on last week really suited him.'

'I can't think why he has to wear a

different one every week,' grumbled Mrs White.

'Shhhh!' said Robbie. 'He's talking about United.'

'. . . a real treat for you tonight. I think we may have seen the birth of one of the great goal-scoring partnerships today, and we definitely have a candidate for *Goal of the Season.*' Chester and Steve sat on the foot of Gran's bed, both of them grinning from ear to ear. The grins disappeared, though, as they watched United being torn apart in the first half. Then at last they saw Chester run onto the pitch.

'Here we go!' said Gran. 'Any moment now you'll see me. Listen! You can hear them chanting. Now watch! Any second you'll see something hit Chester on the head. There!'

Robbie prayed that the TV cameras wouldn't show Barry. 'Something's distracted Smith,' said the commentator. 'The throw-in's been taken quickly though . . .'

'Hey!' said Gran, elbowing herself up off her pillows. 'That's not right! Why don't they show us what's going on in the stand?'

'Calm down!' said Robbie's mum.

'Calm down!' spluttered Gran. 'I wanted

you to see how I dealt with those hooligans. It's not right.' She subsided back into the pillows. Then Chester scored, and everyone in the ward who was able to stand leapt to their feet. Some of them regretted it immediately and collapsed onto their beds with cries of pain. Sister burst in through the swing doors like a tornado.

'Really!' she complained. 'If you cannot be reasonably quiet I shall turn this television off. You may not wish to sleep, but there are other people in the hospital who do!' She caught sight of the slow-motion replay as she spoke. 'Good Lord!' she exclaimed, as Chester's volley crashed into the net. 'That's you!' she said, turning to Chester. 'You're on the telly!'

'Yes!' said Gran. 'That's what we've been trying to tell you.'

The cameras followed Chester as he extracted himself from the pile of players, then cut to a shot of the crowd. Sister's eyes widened in disbelief. 'But that's you, Mrs Devlin!'

'And me!' said Robbie, hopping up and down as if the floor was burning his feet. 'And my friend, Laura! We're on *Match of the Day*!' Someone started to clap and then everyone was clapping and cheering.

'Hold on!' said Chester. 'I want to see this. Oh yes!' On the screen Chester flicked the ball to Steve. 'Go on, Steve!' said Chester, thumping Steve on the back. 'Keep it in! Yes! Now the cross. Perfection!'

'Look at that!' yelled the commentator over the roar of the crowd. 'What a goal!'

All too soon the final whistle blew. 'Quite a game!' said Gary Lineker. 'After the match we managed to catch up with Chester Smith.'

'Extraordinary events here today, Chester,' said the presenter to the cameras. 'You played like a man who's had a weight lifted from his shoulders. A truly spectacular return to form. Now then, before we look at the goals, we've been hearing a lot of rumours that you were looking to leave United. We can forget all that now, I suppose?'

'Well, er, not exactly,' said Chester. 'I've had an offer today, and I'm giving it some serious thought.'

'Well, I'm sure you'll leave a lot of disappointed United fans behind you if you go. They won't forget today's game in a hurry. Talk us through the goals, now . . .'

'Chester?' Robbie said. 'You wouldn't!'

Everyone was staring at Chester. His grin had disappeared.

'Chester?' asked Gran. 'What's going on?'

'I can't stay,' said Chester. 'I wish I could, but I can't. You know why, Robbie. I did warn you.'

'But I thought you'd changed your mind. You said it was fun, helping at school. And you're playing like that. You've got your form back. And those people won't be there any more, not after today. It's not fair to Gran if you go now, not after what she did. You're just giving up. You told me never to give up.'

'I'm sorry,' said Chester. 'I really am. I am having a good time helping out with the team. I'm going to miss you; but I'm going to Italy. I know it's sudden; I didn't expect it. This Italian manager was there to watch Gus Salmon, but he saw me, and he made an offer. It's what I've always wanted. You know that.'

'You're a traitor!' said Robbie. 'I thought you cared about United. But you don't. You only care about yourself!'

Robbie stared miserably at the floor, then Gran gave a shout: 'Look, there, on the telly!'

The TV presenter was explaining just where the defender had gone wrong for Chester's first goal. The picture was frozen, and in the background of the shot the straggling line of troublemakers was being led away.

'That boy!' said Gran. 'That one there. That's our Barry! What's he doing there? What's going on?' Gran began to struggle out of bed. 'I'm not staying here a minute longer. I want to see young Barry. Where is he?'

CHAPTER 15

Sister's patience finally snapped.

'Not one more step, Mrs Devlin,' she said. Gran looked at her, and knew she had met her match. She climbed reluctantly back into bed.

'You can tell Bob to come and fetch me in the morning,' she said, 'and he can bring Barry with him. Then we can have a little chat. "*Didn't want to tire me out!*" You are letting me go in the morning, aren't you, Sister?' Gran made it sound as if she was in prison.

'Just let them try and stop me,' said Sister. 'Now, you lot, out! And as for you . . .' Sister turned to the patients. 'I shall expect to see you all in bed and asleep in two minutes exactly.'

Outside the hospital, Chester said goodbye. Robbie could hardly bear to meet his eyes.

'Barry's not bad,' he said. 'He just doesn't think. He does what his friends do.'

'You could say that about a lot of people,' Chester replied. 'It doesn't make it feel any better when they chuck bananas at you. You don't think: *"It's OK, they're only doing it because their mates do"*.' He saw Robbie's face, miserable in the streetlight. Robbie's mum was looking at him, too. 'Look, I'm sorry,' he continued. 'Not thinking's not good enough, that's all. It hurts people.'

'Barry's sorry,' Robbie told him. 'I know he is. Please don't be angry any more.'

'It's not like that,' said Chester. 'I can't just turn it on and off. I'll see you on Monday.'

'You mean you're coming? But I thought you were going to Italy.'

'It's your big day. I promised, didn't I?'

'I thought . . .'

'Look, what I think about your brother makes no difference to what I think about you. If it wasn't for you I'd probably still be moping around feeling sorry for myself. I might have told Glover to stuff it when he said I was sub; I would have missed my big chance. So I'm going to be there, right? Besides, these things take time. I'll be here till the end of the season. I'm not flying off to Italy tonight, you know.'

They drove in silence for a while, then Robbie said, 'Mum, you do think Dad *will* come and watch on Monday, don't you?'

Mum glanced sideways at Robbie's face, pale in the oncoming headlights. 'He said he'd try,' she said.

'Sometimes I think he hates me. I don't know what I'm supposed to do. I want to be a footballer, I really do; and I can do it – I know I can. Only, when I come home and Dad sneers at me, I feel useless – like it's all a waste of time.'

'That's just silly, love. Of course he doesn't hate you. He's stupid and pig-headed though, sometimes. You know that. He'll come and see you play. I promise you, love; he'll be there.'

Gran stumped up the path early next morning with Dad and Barry trailing behind her. They'd been to fetch her from the hospital. Her right eye was swollen and blackened, and the graze on her cheek was yellowing at the edges.

'Come along, Robbie. We're going to the park. Get your ball.'

'But why . . . ?'

'Barry's coming too, aren't you, Barry? I've decided it's high time I learnt to play football.'

'But Gran, you've just come out of hospital. don't you think . . . ?'

'Stop arguing. Get your ball. I've never felt fitter, and I'm really looking forward to kicking something.' Gran swung her foot and Robbie saw a shiny new trainer flash through the air.

'She made us stop on the way,' said Barry. 'At the supermarket.'

Robbie picked up the ball as Dad brushed past him.

'I give up,' said Dad. 'I just give up.'

'OK,' said Gran, when they reached the end of Woodpecker Drive. 'You might as well get it over with, Barry. No sense hanging about.'

'I'm sorry,' said Barry. 'I'm sorry I messed everything up. I didn't mean to. I wanted to stop it; only I couldn't.'

'I could see,' said Robbie. 'At the match I could see, but there wasn't anything I could do. It all happened so fast.'

'Good,' said Gran. 'That's what I like. Short and to the point. Now let's go and get some dirt on these new trainers.'

'Why now, Gran?' asked Robbie, as they walked towards the rec.

'I was lying in that hospital last night, and I couldn't sleep. I was just turning things over in my mind, thinking about all the great matches I'd been to see. Then I realized; I always used to imagine myself playing. I used to dream about it – Rita Devlin running fifty yards and scoring the winning goal – but I've never kicked a ball in my life. Now if that's not stupid I don't know what is. And then I thought: don't be ridiculous, Rita. You're fifty-five years old; they'll laugh at you. But the more I thought about it, the more I knew I had to do it.'

'Gran,' said Robbie, 'you're amazing!'

Barry went in goal. Gran was impatient to get started, but Robbie made her warm up carefully.

'It's much more important when you're older,' he said. 'You don't want to end up back in hospital, do you?'

Once Gran had warmed up to Robbie's satisfaction, she picked up the ball and placed it on the penalty spot.

'Right,' she said, 'I'm going to enjoy this.'

She ran up to the ball, took a little jump, and a wild kick. The ball trickled forward a few feet. Barry and Robbie burst out laughing together.

'I knew it!' said Gran, and for a second she was angry, but then she began to laugh herself. 'OK, Robbie. You'd better show me what I'm doing wrong.'

Ten minutes later a gang of boys arrived.

'Look at this!' called Darren Peabody, from a safe distance. 'It's that stupid old woman. You playing with an old woman, Barry? You scared of a proper game?'

Gran turned towards them, but Barry was already walking.

'Barry!' said Robbie. 'Where are you going?' Barry didn't reply. When he reached the gang, he stopped.

'I'd rather play with my gran and my brother any day,' he said, 'so just shove off and leave us alone.'

'One little talking-to, and you're a real mummy's boy, aren't you, Barry?' said Shane. 'Your brother thinks he's really something. He didn't stop us getting rid of Smith though, did he?'

'What do you mean, you got rid of him?'

'We,' said Darren. 'You helped, didn't you,

Barry. I bet your Robbie loves you for that.'

Shane took a few steps towards Robbie and Gran. 'Hey, Robbie, you'll be rubbish tomorrow, you'll see. Useless. Come on, Darren, let's go.'

'What did he mean?' asked Barry. 'It's not because of . . . what happened? That's not why Chester's leaving?'

'They didn't make him go,' said Robbie. 'They couldn't – not if he didn't want to. He's going to Italy because that's what he's always wanted, and I bet he'll play for England soon.' Robbie talked on, trying to convince himself it was true. 'Just think,' he went on, 'we'll know an England player.'

'I won't,' said Barry. All the things he had said about Chester seemed ridiculous now. Chester could have been his friend, too.

'You'll meet him properly tomorrow,' said Gran, 'when you come and watch Robbie play in the tournament. Now then, let's get on with this game.'

Robbie played on, but his heart wasn't in it. He had never expected Chester to leave. He'd imagined him going on playing for United for years. Maybe Chester would have fixed him up with a trial at United. Robbie had even imagined himself in a few years' time, running out onto the North

Park pitch with Chester and Steve. That wasn't going to happen now; but what about the rest of it? What about the tournament tomorrow? The others didn't believe in him, not really; he'd heard them. And Robbie, suddenly, wasn't sure if he believed in himself.

Dad didn't even mention the tournament the next morning. He overslept and dashed out of the house with a piece of toast in one hand and his briefcase in the other. It ought to have been a good day for Robbie, but it wasn't. People wanted to talk to him, asking about the United game. Some of them had even spotted him on the TV. Laura kept going on about it, every chance she got, but all Robbie could think about was the sick feeling in his stomach. He just wanted to be on his own. His legs were jelly. He wouldn't be able to run, let alone kick a football.

At lunchtime, Robbie sat by himself on a bench. He saw the rest of the team in a huddle, talking. He saw them looking at him, and he could guess what they were saying. He knew he didn't look much like a footballer, sitting there feeling sick. He started to hope something would happen and the competition would be called off, but the rest of the day went past in a blur. All too soon they were on the minibus heading for the Sports Centre on the other side of town.

Through the steamed-up minibus window, Robbie gazed at a huge sweep of bright green Astroturf, shining in the floodlights. Teams were already warming up. At the edge of the car park he saw Chester, surrounded by reporters and photographers. When Chester saw them he pushed through the crowd and joined them. He shook Miss MacGregor's hand and grinned.

'I think you'll get all the publicity you want now,' he said. 'You lot go and get changed and I'll meet you on the pitch.'

As soon as Robbie came out of the building, he saw Gran. She was wearing her United scarf. Mum and Barry were with her. Robbie ran over to them.

'Where's Dad?' he asked. 'Has he come?'

'It's early yet,' said Mum. 'Give him time. You look very nice in your . . . whatever it is.'

Gran snorted. 'It's a strip,' she said. 'That's what it's called. Yellow and green, like Brazil. Robbie, you shouldn't be here.

You should be over there with the team, warming up.'

One look at Gran's face told Robbie she knew just how he was feeling.

'Go on,' she said, 'you can do it. They're waiting.'

CHAPTER 16

Sixteen teams had entered the tournament, and the draw had already been made. In the first round Field View 'A' were to play Market Gates Middle School. They were out on the pitch now, wearing a strip of gold and black stripes. As he looked around Robbie realized what a lot of people had turned up to watch this competition. He looked at the floodlights and the crisp green pitch with its immaculate white markings. He looked at the low, gleaming six-a-side goals with their orange nets, and he felt all his doubts return in force. He juggled a ball half-heartedly with one foot as the others talked.

'Scary, isn't it?' Max said.

'Yeah,' Jake agreed, 'I didn't expect all

these people. And that Market Gates team look really good.'

Martin and Nicky looked worried too. Only Ian seemed confident.

'OK,' Chester told them, 'you don't worry about them. And you don't worry about this crowd either. You concentrate on doing what we've practised. Pass and move. Keep it simple. You'll run rings around them. Hey, Robbie, you listening or what?'

Robbie hadn't heard a word Chester had said. He'd been scanning the crowd, looking for Dad. He couldn't see him anywhere. Mr Pitt was there, though; standing alone on the touchline, trying to look important.

'Come on, Robbie,' said Chester, 'snap out of it. We need you, right?' Robbie forced himself to smile and nod. Inside he knew that everything was going to go wrong.

Jake was the captain. He won the toss, and chose to kick off. Ian passed to Jake, and the moment the ball was in play Robbie knew that he simply didn't want it. He knew that if the ball came to him, he'd make a mistake. It was a certainty, like a stone in the pit of his stomach. And there was no escape, because he knew that in two seconds' time Jake would be laying the ball back to him, the way they'd practised dozens of times.

Robbie heard the voices yelling from the touchline, and in among them, as Jake played the pass, he was sure he heard Shane yelling, *'Useless!'*. He glanced over; he couldn't stop himself. Shane wasn't there; he'd imagined it, and suddenly the ball was at his feet.

Robbie controlled it, but slowly – far too slowly. A black-and-gold attacker was thundering down at him like a steam train, and Robbie did the only thing he could; he played it back to Nicky Slater. Nicky was taken by surprise. This wasn't how they'd planned it. He pushed the ball forward, but the attacker was on him and the ball ricocheted out for a Market Gates throw.

'Come on, Robbie,' said Jake. 'Wake up.'

'Sorry,' muttered Robbie, as the throw was taken. An attacker was on to the ball in a flash and drove a shot at Max's goal. Max dived low to his left and grabbed the ball solidly with both hands. Without a pause, he rolled it to Martin, the other defender.

Chester had told them, 'Get the ball out quickly if you can. You might catch them napping.' He was right. Martin spotted Jake at once, moving forward into space on

157

the right hand side. The pass was good. Jake controlled it neatly, stopped and turned, looking for Robbie running in support – but Robbie wasn't there. Jake turned again, looking desperately for someone to pass to, but he turned into trouble. The Market Gates defender had managed to get back, and the chance was gone.

At half-time Jake said to Robbie, 'Where were you? We won't catch them like that again. It was a brilliant chance.'

Robbie looked away. This was a nightmare and he just wanted it to end.

'You're doing OK,' Chester said to them. 'Keep plugging away and you'll get a goal.' Robbie could hear the disappointment in his voice. Chester didn't look at him.

The second half began, and Robbie discovered how easy it was not to touch the ball. The rest of the team had lost confidence in him. They weren't keen to pass to him anyway, but Robbie made sure they didn't have the chance. Just as he instinctively knew where to run to receive a pass, so he managed to find the places on the pitch where there was no chance of him getting the ball. Field View might as well have been playing with five players. Even so they won the game, thanks to a brilliant goal scored by Ian. He beat two defenders before sliding the ball into the net, but Robbie hardly noticed. There was a cold silence from the others when the match ended. Chester congratulated them, then he took Robbie to one side.

'What do you think you're doing?' he said. 'All this work for nothing. How could you do that?'

'You can talk,' said Robbie. 'It's happened to you too, hasn't it? Well now I know what it's like, and I wish I didn't.'

'Yeah, sure,' said Chester. 'It's happened to me. It happens to everybody. But just because I was an idiot doesn't give you the right. You think about the others, Robbie. You think about the kids who could have played, but we gave you the chance. Just stop feeling sorry for yourself, will you?'

'But I don't know what to do. It's this feeling . . . if the ball comes my way I just know I'm going to make a mess of it.'

'You've got to focus. There's nothing out there but you and the ball and the players. You know what it's like when it's going well. Think about it. Remember it.'

'But the others. They think I'm a—'

'The first time you do something special

they'll forget all about it. Right now, they won't pass to you if they can help it. You can't expect them to. You'll have to fight for the ball. You'll have to win their respect back. I'm not saying it'll be easy, but that's what you've got to do, Robbie.'

In his head, Robbie heard Dad's voice – *'Practise, practise, practise, that's all you ever do. I'd like to see what you make of a real match.'* He could just imagine what Dad would say if he saw him now. He looked up and caught sight of Mr Pitt. He knew what *he* was thinking. Robbie felt a sudden surge of anger, and the anger seemed to burn the sickness away from his stomach. He stood up and walked over to where the others were talking to Miss MacGregor and Mr Osborne.

'I'm sorry,' he said. 'I was rubbish, but I'll be OK now.'

The others looked at him doubtfully, as a man with a loud hailer called them onto the pitch for their next game.

This time Jake lost the toss. The other team were playing in blue, and they were good. That was obvious right away. They passed the ball around neatly and everyone on the Field View team had to work hard to prevent them threatening Max's goal.

Robbie lost himself in the job of marking, and he did it well, but still the others on his own side didn't pass to him.

When his chance came, it came suddenly. One of the blue attackers lost his marker for a second and managed to hit a fierce shot at goal. Nicky Slater had seen the danger and launched himself desperately in an attempt to block the shot. The ball hit his outstretched boot and flew towards Robbie like a bullet. Robbie acted instinctively, killing the ball, already half turning, looking for an incisive pass.

Jake hadn't moved. He was expecting Robbie to fluff it, but when he saw the brilliant way Robbie controlled the ball he began to run. Jake wasn't quite where he should have been when the pass came. He had to stretch to reach the ball and all he could do was to push it away from the defender, but that was enough. Martin had seen what was happening and made a run down the touchline, anticipating where Jake would push the ball. He ran past the last defender and pulled the ball back for Ian to smash it into the net.

Jake climbed to his feet. 'About time,' he said to Robbie. Then he smiled. 'I'll be ready for the next one.'

From that moment, Field View's passing and movement were unstoppable, and Robbie was at the heart of it all. Good though the opposition were, and hard though they worked, they couldn't stop Field View scoring two more goals, one from Jake and one from Ian.

There were no special congratulations for Robbie from Chester when the game was over.

'Well done, everyone,' he said. 'You're playing like a team at last. But you've got to remember, it's easy to lose your concentration after playing like that. I bet you all think you're as good as in the Final already.' Chester might have been a mind-reader. Robbie was already imagining them collecting the trophy.

'You've got two more games to win first,' Chester said. 'You can do it, but you've got to concentrate. Go on. The ref wants you.'

The semi-final was uncomfortably close. In the first half, neither side managed a single shot on goal. Then, soon after the second half began, Field View went behind when a cross was deflected and spun into the corner of Max's goal. Somehow Field View couldn't recapture the devastating form of the previous game, and as the minutes ticked away, their heads began to drop.

'Come on!' yelled Chester. 'Pass and move. Be patient. Don't give the ball away!'

Robbie was on the ball. Everywhere he looked players were tightly marked. Out of the corner of his eye he saw the ref look at his watch, then he heard Max's voice.

'Here, Robbie!'

Max had raced out of his goal, causing confusion among the opposition. Robbie slipped the ball to him, and as a defender left Jake to challenge Max, Max threaded a beautiful pass to Jake, who at last found himself free to run at the goal. He made no mistake, and in the final second the scores were level. There would be penalties.

Chester gave them their instructions. 'Keep the ball on the ground and make sure you get it on target. That way you've got a chance. If you miss you've got none. Jake, you take the first one.'

Robbie felt relief wash over him when Chester told him he'd take the last penalty. One way or the other it was sure to be decided before then. He was wrong. The tension rose as shot after shot hit the back of the net, until both teams had scored four penalties, and each had just one shot left.

Robbie stood waiting for the ref's whistle. He fought to control his racing heart, but he could feel the blood pounding in his ears. He thought of nothing except the place where the ball was going to go. Then, suddenly, he imagined himself back in the alley, aiming at a target on the wall, and as the whistle blew he felt completely calm. He stepped up and hit the shot, inch perfect, shaving the inside of the post.

Robbie hardly heard the congratulations as Max took his place in the goal. He only had to save this and they were through. It was a game of bluff. Max had dived to the left every time, and every time so far he'd been wrong. Robbie couldn't watch. He covered his eyes. He heard the whistle, and the thud of a foot on the ball, and then all the players around him were cheering. Robbie looked. Max had dived left again, but this time he'd guessed right. He was holding the ball in his hands as if he was never going to let it go.

CHAPTER 17

'That was brilliant,' said Chester. 'If you can fight like that in the final, you'll have no trouble.'

'Chester,' said Jake, 'don't you think Robbie could play further forward? It's just . . . I think . . . we all think he'd score goals. You know how he can shoot. And you saw how he took that penalty.'

'What is this?' said Chester. 'A mutiny?'

Robbie couldn't believe his ears. He'd seen them talking after the semi-final finished, while he was with Mum and Gran, but this was the last thing he'd expected.

'What do you think, Robbie?' asked Chester. 'You play further forward, and Jake drops back. You link up with Ian every chance you get. Shoot on sight.'

Robbie looked at the waiting faces; there was no doubt in their eyes, not any more.

'Great,' he said. 'We'll have to try something different if we're going to beat this lot.'

The City Road team didn't just look big; they looked mean. They had beaten the Field View 'B' team in the second round, and they were a team Mr Pitt would have approved of. Every one of the 'B' team had bruises to show from their own encounter with City Road.

Jake shook hands with the City Road captain. He lost the toss, and City Road kicked off. Robbie had expected them to be hard, but he hadn't expected them to attack with such speed. For a crucial few moments the whole Field View team were asleep, and when those few moments were over, it was too late. A cry of 'Goal!!' burst from the supporters on the touchline, and there was Max flat on his face and the ball in the back of the net. 1–0 to City Road and only thirty seconds gone!

'This is going to be a walkover!' said the City Road captain to his friend as Ian placed the ball on the centre spot.

'That's what you think,' muttered Robbie. His vision had cleared. It had been a shaky moment, but there was no way he wanted to relive the nightmare of the first game.

'Come on,' he shouted, 'let's get at them!'

Jake looked at him, surprised by the determination in his voice. 'Right!' he responded, clapping his hands. 'You heard Robbie. We can do it.'

Ian kicked off. Robbie began to run, looking for the empty spaces through which Jake would be threading the ball at any moment. He felt a boot connect with his shin, and found himself dumped onto the rough surface of the pitch. The ball ran harmlessly through to the City Road goal-keeper.

'Foul!' shouted Robbie, looking round angrily for the player who had tripped him. A boy with a fat face and little piggy blue eyes stood near him, grinning. The whistle didn't blow.

'Hey, ref!' called Ian. 'Didn't you see that? He tripped him up.'

'Play on!' said the referee. 'Come along, keep the game moving!'

As Robbie picked himself up a City Road player ran past with the ball. Another pass and a boy with curly red hair was running towards Max's goal with only Martin to beat. Martin stood in front of him, watching the ball closely. The red-haired boy tried to go past Martin on the outside, but he wasn't quick enough, and Martin played the ball safely out over the touchline, just the way Chester had trained him. The red-haired boy tripped and fell. The whistle blew, and the referee ran up, panting and dragging his feet.

'Well done, Martin!' Jake called out. 'Brilliant!'

'Foul!' said the referee. 'Free kick to City Road!'

'Come off it, ref,' yelled Gran from the touchline. 'Get yourself a pair of glasses!'

'Now then, Mrs Devlin,' said Miss MacGregor, 'we must respect the referee's decisions. We want our school to have a reputation for fair play.'

'Fair play, my eye!' retorted Gran. 'That ref's not playing fair. He's blind as a bat!'

Barry edged nearer to Chester. 'Mr Smith?' he said.

'In a minute, all right?' said Chester. 'I'm watching the game.'

'Please,' Barry said, 'I know you're angry with me, but I just wanted you to know; I never knew they were going to do that, at the match, I mean.'

Chester looked at Barry as the City Road players argued over who was going to take the free kick. 'So when I met you at school, and you didn't want to talk to me, that wasn't your fault either?'

Barry reddened. 'I was wrong,' he said. 'I was stupid. I'm sorry.'

'Barry!' said Dad. 'What's going on? They're all standing around. Nothing's happening. Oh . . .' he said, as he saw Chester, 'it's you. I . . .'

'I met you, didn't I?' Chester said. 'In that park. You're Robbie's dad.'

'Oh . . . well . . . that was all a stupid mistake, wasn't it? Could have happened to anybody. No hard feelings, eh?'

'Not for you, maybe. Now, if it's all the same to you, I'd like to watch the game.' Chester turned away.

For a moment it looked as if Dad was about to say something else. Barry tugged at his jacket. 'Mum's over here,' he said. As they walked away, Chester called after them, 'Thanks, Barry. You're all right.'

'What did he mean by that?' asked Dad.

'Nothing,' Barry replied. 'You wouldn't understand.'

*　　*　　*

The referee blew his whistle impatiently.

'Go on, Masher,' shouted the red-haired boy. 'Smash it in!'

Piggy-eyes ran up. The ball flew like a guided missile, but Max was airborne as well, and his flying, outstretched fingers just touched the ball over the bar. The whistle blew. 'Goal kick!' said the ref.

'Oh, Ref!' said Piggy-eyes. 'He saved it! It's a corner.'

'Now, now, lad. The referee is always right, remember?'

As the game went on the Field View team found themselves tripped or pushed constantly whenever the referee wasn't looking. Then, at last, a real chance came their way. Nicky robbed the red-headed boy of the ball deep in the Field View half of the field. He looked up quickly and spotted Jake in plenty of space near the centre circle, so he hit a pass to him, hard and low. Jake controlled the ball carefully and turned, looking for the attackers running ahead of him. Robbie checked suddenly, jumped over the outstretched foot of the defender, and called to Jake for the ball. He had his back to goal, but he knew instinctively what Ian would be expecting him to do, and when the ball arrived he gave it a delicate flick with the outside of his left foot. His touch completely deceived the defenders, and the instant he had played the ball he spun away in the opposite direction, heading for the spot where he knew that Ian would place the return pass. There was a crash, and a sudden blackness, as if he had run into a brick wall. Robbie felt himself falling . . .

'. . . Robbie! Robbie? Are you all right, Robbie?'

Robbie opened his eyes and saw Dad's face looking down at him. For a second he thought he was dreaming, but his head hurt too much for that. He sat up slowly.

'Dad. You came.'

'And a good job, too,' said Dad. 'You'd better come over here and sit down. That was a nasty crack. I could have sworn that lad swung his elbow on purpose. You've got a substitute, haven't you?'

Robbie stood up. 'You must be joking,' he said. 'I'm not coming off now. I'm going to take the free kick.'

'Oh, I'm sorry, lad,' said the referee, 'but I'm sure it was an accident, you know.'

'My sainted aunt!' exclaimed Gran, who had come on to the pitch to make sure

Robbie was all right. 'If that was an accident, I'm Bobby Charlton!'

Robbie looked at Dad's worried face. Tears stung his eyes.

'Thanks, Dad,' he said, 'I'm glad you came.'

'Well, like I said, it's a good job I did. Who's in charge of this lot?' He looked at the referee. 'Is it you? Well then, you tell him. He's not fit to carry on.'

'Dad!' Robbie blinked back the tears. 'Can't you see? That's not what I want; just leave it, all right?'

He turned and ran back on to the pitch. The referee was looking worried. 'It's OK,' said Gran. 'Anyone can see he's fine. And as for you,' she added, turning to Dad, 'all you have to do is say "Well done". Otherwise you keep your big mouth shut.'

The game re-started. Ian played the ball to Robbie; as the others ran, he saw space open up in front of him. All he had to do was beat Piggy-eyes.

'Come on, then!' jeered Piggy-eyes, and he planted his feet wide apart, ready to trip Robbie if he tried to go past him. Robbie saw his chance. He pushed the ball neatly between Piggy-eyes' legs, and saw his jaw drop as he slipped around him. He had all the time in the world; Piggy-eyes was rooted to the spot. There was only the goalkeeper to beat, and Robbie didn't hesitate. Before Piggy-eyes had time to move he sent his shot sizzling low into the left-hand corner of the net. On the touchline, the spectators went crazy as the referee blew the whistle for half time.

'Are you sure you're all right?' asked Dad as Robbie came off the pitch.

'Bob!' said Mum.

'You've got them rattled now,' said Chester.

'Brilliant,' said Laura.

'We're going to win, aren't we?' Barry added.

'I wish I was playing,' said Gran.

'So do I, Madam,' put in Mr Osborne. 'I haven't enjoyed myself so much for ages.'

The second half began. Robbie felt confidence surging through him, and when City Road kicked off, he shot forward immediately to intercept a pass, then curled the ball out to Jake on the left wing. Jake pushed the ball past a defender and sprinted forward, leaving him floundering behind him. He looked up and saw Robbie racing towards the edge of the penalty area.

173

Robbie watched the ball flashing towards him. He heard voices yelling from the touch-line, all mixed together: Mum and Chester, Gran and Barry, Mr Osborne and Miss MacGregor, Laura; even Dad was shouting now. And he knew what he was going to do. This wasn't for Dad; it wasn't for Chester; it wasn't for any of them; it was just for him. As the ball floated towards him he flung himself backwards. His spinning right foot intersected perfectly with the flight of the ball and slammed it past the despairing fingers of the goalkeeper . . .

THE END

BROOKSIE
by Neil Arksey

*Imagine being the son of one of England's
top strikers . . . Great, yes!*

No! Not if, like Lee Brooks, your dad –
'Brooksie' – has suddenly lost form and
become the laughing-stock of the
whole country.

Lee hates Brooksie for letting him down.
And Lee hates having to move to a grotty
new home without his dad. With his own on-
pitch confidence at an all-time low, he even
begins to hate *football*. But then he meets
Dent and his mates and the chance is there
for him to play again – with a team of
seriously talented players. They've
just one problem – no pitch!

A cracking football tale, filled with goal-
scoring and dramatic matchplay moments.

ISBN 0 440 863813

CORGI YEARLING BOOKS

FOOTBALL MAGIC
by Elizabeth Dale

*The competition's really tough – everyone
wants to go on Football Magic!*

Andy, Paul and Leroy are the best soccer
players in their schools. That's why they're
on the Football Magic course. But what is a
wimpy looking boy like Dave doing there?
He's not like the rest of them. He doesn't
boast about his talents for a start. AND he
keeps sticking up for girls. Just because his
sister scored the winning goal in the Inter-
Schools Cup, doesn't mean girls are any
good at football, does it?

But Dave has something to prove, and once
he gets on the pitch his skills do all the
talking. He's magic! But what will everyone
think when they learn his secret?

End-to-end action on and off the pitch in
this great soccer story!

ISBN 0 440 863589

CORGI YEARLING BOOKS